Puffin Books

STAN

The early hours of a warm September morning are shattered by the sound of police sirens. Lying in bed, planning his escape from an uncaring London foster home to join his older brother in Ireland, Stan little realizes the fateful connection between him and the commotion outside.

Later that day, the burly fourteen-year-old hitches north from London, only to find himself being pursued, not by the welfare authorities as he'd expected, but by a desperate criminal. He soon realizes that the dubiously named Julius Lodge will stop at nothing to get what he wants, and Stan has it!

From London to Warrington and Liverpool, then by ferry to Ireland, Stan always manages to evade Julius's clutches. But all the while, more powerful than his fear, is his determination to find his real home and not be taken back to London. Across the Irish Sea, however, an even greater danger than Julius confronts him before he can reach his brother.

This powerful and gripping thriller is also the story of a boy's lonely but extraordinarily courageous search for a place in a warm and loving family. With all the raw emotion and originality that won for *Henry's Leg* the *Guardian* Award for Children's Fiction (and made it a successful television series), and which attracted high praise for *The Year of the Worm* and *The Big Pink*, Ann Pilling has, in *Stan*, written an exciting and yet deeply moving story.

Ann Pilling was born in W... trial north-west. She studie... and subsequently became... Oxford and is married wit...

Also by Ann Pilling

THE BIG PINK
HENRY'S LEG
THE YEAR OF THE WORM

ANN PILLING

Stan

PUFFIN BOOKS

PUFFIN BOOKS

Published by the Penguin Group
Penguin Books Ltd, 27 Wrights Lane, London W8 5TZ, England
Penguin Books USA Inc., 375 Hudson Street, New York, New York 10014, USA
Penguin Books Australia Ltd, Ringwood, Victoria, Australia
Penguin Books Canada Ltd, 10 Alcorn Avenue, Toronto, Ontario, Canada M4V 3B2
Penguin Books (NZ) Ltd, 182–190 Wairau Road, Auckland 10, New Zealand

Penguin Books Ltd, Registered Offices: Harmondsworth, Middlesex, England

First published by Viking Kestrel 1988
Published in Puffin Books 1989
10 9 8 7 6 5 4 3

The author and publisher gratefully acknowledge permission from
Macmillan London Ltd to quote the opening eight lines of 'The Bright Field'
from *Laboratories of the Spirit* by R. S. Thomas, and from Faber and Faber Ltd
to quote from 'To My Mother' from *Collected Poems* by George Barker

Printed in England by Clays Ltd, St Ives plc
Filmset in Linotron 202 Palatino

for Gina Pollinger,
one of the real people

I have seen the sun break through
To illuminate a small field
For a while, and gone my way
and forgotten it. But that was the pearl
Of great price, the one field that had
the treasure in it. I realise now
that I must give all I have
to possess it.

R. S. Thomas
(from 'The Bright Field')

Chapter One

Stan stirred in his sleep then woke suddenly and sat up. 'Kingsley? You awake?'

The hump in the other bed didn't budge. But something had waked him, a noise several streets away that had ripped open the darkness and into his dream. Was it a car backfiring? Perhaps. He couldn't tell, not at this distance.

There was a clock on the small cupboard between the beds. It wasn't his, his half-sister Elspeth had brought it with her. It showed Noddy and Big-Ears in a garden of flowers. As the seconds ticked away Noddy's head moved in rhythm, idiotically. Stan hadn't got a watch so he'd pinched the clock just for tonight. He had to be away by five, to be sure.

The yellow hands were at three o'clock. The sound came again but this time it was nearer. Who could be driving round the streets at this time of night in an old banger? Someone would cop it next day.

Silence spread out again and there were no more noises. Perhaps they already had, Stan thought.

He lay back and dropped his hand to feel in the space between the bed and the cupboard. His rucksack was there with his anorak folded on top, just as he'd left it, so for once Kingsley hadn't been snooping.

It was early September but very mild still with summer hanging on. The sash-window between the beds was wide open on to the airless London night and there was a moon, bright enough to cast bars of shadow on to the lino. Stan undid his pyjama jacket and pulled at his sweater for air. He was fully clothed under the covers, the pyjamas had been for Kingsley's benefit. He was too nosy for his own good, that one.

The minutes passed. Noddy's head rocked to and fro crazily and Stan shut his eyes, taking deep breaths of the stale stuffy air, trying to grab back at sleep. He'd only got two hours left. How long would it be before he slept in a bed again?

Then the night exploded. The cracking noise started up again but much nearer, splitting the darkness. The houses rang with it and there were car engines revving madly and footsteps hammering the pavement, and people shouting. Then a police car wailed up from far away and under his head, two floors down, a dog started yapping.

Kingsley's mound was stirring slightly when the bedroom door was flung open and a man came in. Stan opened his eyes to a slit, not enough to show he was awake but enough to see Victor.

All he could make out was the black silhouette of a small thin figure half his own size. He could smell him though; a faint cigar smoke, tweed, the whiff of aftershave. Only one person had that expensive smell in this house, Victor McCann, Kingsley's father and the husband of the woman Stan called 'Auntie Marjorie', the woman who fostered him.

The police car sounded close now, and the dog was barking wildly.

'For *Christ's sake*!' the man was hissing through clenched teeth.

The yellowish light through the thin curtains shone on a wild face. The man's mouth was open and full of spit. He was looking round the room frantically, his piggy eyes bloodshot and bulging with panic. He ran one hand aimlessly through his limp black hair then clutched it into a greasy lump, as if he was trying to pull his own head off. *Concentrate, Victor boy*. At the bottom of the house the dog barked again and there was a muffled thumping sound.

Victor pulled at the curtains. The thin wire that held them in place came away and everything flopped on the floor. He straddled the sill and looked out.

Stan thought he'd gone when the man suddenly turned and dropped back into the room. He looked from bed to bed and hesitated, then he was on his knees by the cupboard. Stan could smell the sweat of fear on top of the after-shave. He was ramming something soft and squishy down into hiding somewhere, no doubt into one of the many cracks in the skirting in the decayed house.

Then he disappeared. Stan watched as he swung himself over the window-ledge and heard dull thuds as the small man moved expertly down the outside wall from the attic room. There was a faint crunch as his feet flattened down the first crisp eddies of dead leaves that had swilled up round the dustbins. Then silence.

Stan sat up in bed and peered out. The line of long narrow city gardens stretched in a pattern to the end of the terrace, dim rectangles of grey, like so many coffins. Victor was threading his way along the back walls. Stan could see the orange of his padded ski-jacket in the haze from the street lights. It was a perfect target. The man was paying now for his taste in flashy clothes.

The boy lost him in a jumble of sheds and garages but he stayed at the window, listening hard. The dog stopped barking, then he heard the thump of their front door. Several cars roared off together, sirens wailing, fading finally into the night. Then dark figures appeared behind the houses, stumbling from garden to garden, smashing into fences and cold-frames with heavy boots, flashing torches. They had dogs and they were going Victor's way.

'Kingsley? You awake?' Stan tried again but the

mound was snoring now. He lay back and waited for someone to come up to them. But nobody showed up, not even Auntie Marjorie.

He shut his eyes, the night settled down again and silence took over. Perhaps he'd dreamed it. Now, when it was so near dawn and he'd have to get moving, he felt real sleep coming.

He was awake again just after five. Noddy's illuminated head still waggled like a zombie on the flowered face of Elspeth's clock. It would be typical of Kingsley to wake up now and see him so he got out of bed very slowly, took the pyjama jacket off and fastened himself into his anorak. The zip noise sounded horribly loud in the stillness but Kingsley didn't budge, even though Stan waited. With his boots in one hand and his rucksack in the other he started to move very slowly, down through the sleeping house. Auntie Marjorie's door was open and the bed a tumble of empty sheets.

Elspeth hadn't got a proper bedroom; she slept in a kind of cubby-hole off one of the landings. In spite of the smell Stan went in.

She lay half in, half out of the bed, sweetly asleep, as he stared down at her. She was quite pretty really, but very pale and transparent-looking, as if she was made of fish and chips, and her hands felt cold. Stan covered her up carefully, disturbing the big orange cat which was curled up in a neat tight circle on her feet.

And suddenly he didn't want to go at all; he knelt down by the bed and buried his face in the ginger fur. The cat stretched and opened the circle obligingly, it knew Stan, and a slow purr began, deep inside.

Dawn was coming, the house filling slowly with that first grey chill. But it was warm here with Fat Cat. What was he doing, leaving? He was off his head. He could go back, even now, he could go straight back upstairs and get into bed.

But it was time, and he wasn't going to chicken out

12

now, change his mind yet again and play safe. He'd done that once too often, hoping things might get better, but they never had. So he stood up and put the note he'd written the night before on top of Elspeth's clothes, by the bed. She couldn't read very well so he'd done it in big printing. 'Dear Elspeth,' it said, 'Look after Fat Cat till I get back. Lots of love, Stan.'

Down in the kitchen, where he'd planned to leave his other note, he found a piece of paper propped up against the cornflakes packet. It was his foster-mother's writing and it had obviously been scribbled in a great hurry. 'Boys,' it said, 'Get yourselves to school. Janice will collect Elspeth at 8.30. *Don't go till she has.* Lock up. I'll be back tonight at the usual time. Love, Mum.'

Stan stared at it and remembered the thumping noise in the middle of the night, the noise that had set the dog off. The police must have come and taken her away with them, to answer questions. She'd not put it in the note.

She didn't really have to. That's where she was.

He hadn't thought leaving would be so hard. Elspeth had only come a few weeks ago and there'd been violent rows about her with Victor ever since. But when Stan thought about her asleep in the cubby-hole, waking up to Kingsley, not him, he felt choked. And the letter he'd just put on the table had been hard to write too.

English and writing were what he was best at. When he left school he'd quite like to be a reporter and work on a big newspaper. Finding the right words for this though had been impossible, like squeezing blood out of a stone.

His first effort had started 'Dear Mrs McCann', but he'd changed that, it was too cruel. She was his foster-mother and he'd lived with her for nearly four years. She'd asked him to call her 'Auntie Marjorie' so he had.

It wasn't her fault but she'd never felt like one; there'd been too many 'aunties' in Stan's life, whole armies of them, all shapes and sizes, in homes and foster homes and temporary 'care' centres. No one of his own though. Mrs Kelly had never said 'Call me Auntie' and he never had, not once. But they'd loved each other. What did it matter what you called people anyway?

'Dear Auntie Marjorie,' he'd written finally, 'I'm sorry but I'm leaving. I was going to hang on and wait for a bit but I can't take any more. I'm sorry. Please will you explain to Elspeth and I'll write when I'm settled. Thanks for everything. Love, Stan.'

In the back kitchen Carl, Kingsley's Alsatian, gave a throaty growl when it saw him, then its tail started thumping. Stan patted him. 'Goodbye, dog, I wish I could take you with me.' The big soft animal rolled on its back hopefully, ready to play. There was a knobbly lump in Stan's throat but he swallowed it down, and turned away.

The two pieces of paper stood propped against the cornflakes packet, one at each end. It was just too bad that his carefully laid plans had come to a head tonight of all nights. Perhaps he should explain to Auntie Marjorie that he'd not actually planned it that way. He put his hand out to take his note back, and felt on the cluttered sideboard for something to write with.

But somebody was moving about upstairs. Was it Victor's drinking companion, the man who called himself Julius Lodge? He'd arrived three nights ago and kipped down in the little box-room half-way up the first staircase. Stan hadn't dared look in there. Quickly he swung the rucksack up on to his back, pushed his feet into his boots and knotted them rapidly. Then he straightened up and looked at the ceiling. Someone was definitely awake, and moving about over his head.

He left his note where it was and slipped out silently.

Chapter Two

Daylight. Stan was sitting in a shed on the edge of some allotments a bare mile from home. His boots felt heavy. Walking here from the house, down alley-ways and along the backs of gardens, keeping well away from roads, his feet had dragged like stone lumps. He wished now he'd put ordinary shoes on and not the heavy walking boots he'd found at a jumble sale.

But he'd thought it all out. He might have to do a lot of walking in the next few weeks. These boots would come into their own then.

He ate a pork pie and a few biscuits, then drank a can of Coke. He hadn't brought much with him, because of the weight, and he'd saved money for food anyway. Now Victor was on the run, though, going into shops might be a bit dodgy.

The police would be on the look-out for a missing boy. They always were and they nearly always found them and brought them back. It'd happened twice to other kids when Stan was in the short-stay place between Mrs Kelly's and Auntie Marjorie's.

For months now he'd been lying low, watching and weighing things up, just quietly biding his time. There was no point in running off before he was ready, they'd only find him. Now though he thought he could make it.

Stan was fourteen but people thought he was older because he was very tall and chunky-looking. The thing you noticed straight away was his hair. When he pulled off his knitted woollen hat a shower of fair curls tumbled out. It was so thick and curly and such a bright straw colour that everyone looked twice. With hair like that showing you'd recognize him at once.

His half-brother, Sid, had the same kind of springy hair only a bit darker. Stan hadn't seen him for nearly two years now, but every time they met he seemed so much bigger. They definitely looked like brothers. Sid was just an older, taller version of Stan but with a longer face and a sharper nose and chin. Take away the jeans and the dirty face, and the farmyard smell, Sid was half-way between a young giant and a Greek god. Stan thought he was great.

That was where he was making for, Ireland, where Sid was, in a place called County Cork, learning to be a farmer with Mrs Kelly's brother, Joe. The old lady had kept her promise. As soon as he'd finished with school Sid had taken off, just like he always said he would. He was old enough so they couldn't stop him.

Stan had missed him a lot. It wouldn't have been so bad if he'd still had Mrs Kelly looking after him, but they'd taken her into hospital and dumped him in one of those temporary care places. He'd got the social worker to give him the address of the farm in County Cork and now they wrote letters to each other.

Sid wasn't much good at it, not a patch on Stan. He held a pen like a screwdriver and filled the paper with smudges and crossings out; but now and again he sent little notes, in brown envelopes with Irish stamps. There was money in them sometimes, from Mrs Kelly's brother, big Irish pounds covered with funny little drawings, a lot better than English pound coins. When he'd saved five Auntie Marjorie changed them for him at the bank, and he kept the fivers in a plastic bag. No one had told him to save the money but he always did. It was part of his plan.

A typical Sid letter would be something like this: 'Dear Stan, Everything's great here, and hope this finds you the same. Here's something for you to spend, from Joe. I'll be coming over to see you one of these days. Cheers. Sid.'

He'd never actually said 'Come out and join me' but he didn't have to. They were brothers, weren't they, and they'd only had each other, all the years they'd been growing up. They'd not had fights either, not like some kids. Stan knew it'd be OK if he just turned up one day at Joe's farm, out of the blue. He didn't have any doubts on that score.

He'd been careful not to leave any of Sid's letters at Auntie Marjorie's because the name of the town in Ireland was stamped on the envelope. Sid never wrote an address but the town would be all the police needed, to track him down. Stan had torn off a bit with the postmark on and stuck it for safety at the back of his red notebook.

He knew he ought to get out of the shed now and start walking, but he couldn't make himself, not yet. Instead he slid his notebook out of the rucksack and started looking through it. Miss Dobbs, tall, slender, sweet-smelling, a kind of human willow tree in ethnic gypsy dresses and a cloud of soft auburn hair, would be on her way to school by now, with *him*. She'd never know that she'd been the last straw.

'This term,' she'd told his class last week, giving out brand-new books, 'we're going to read an anthology. Now does anybody know what that is?'

Nobody knew except Stan but he wasn't putting his hand up. He'd learned long ago in that set-up to act pretty dim in public. If you showed you were actually interested in lessons you always suffered afterwards, especially with something like English. It was a good thing he was sporty, and OK on the football field, other-

17

wise, with the praise Miss Dobbs heaped on him sometimes for the things he wrote, he'd seem a real pansy.

She never gave up with Class 4B. 'Years ago,' she'd
explained patiently, when no one had come up with an
answer, 'you might have made your own notebook, if
you could read and write that is. People did it all the
time, they copied out things they'd read and wanted to
remember. Sometimes they'd write things themselves.
These collections were personal anthologies, if you like,
they were called "Commonplace Books".' (Silence in the
form room, then bored shuffling.)

'It's something you could do yourselves, perhaps,'
she'd gone on brightly. 'All you need is an ordinary notebook.'

People in the back row had started talking, they
weren't in the least interested. They don't deserve a
fabulous teacher like Miss Dobbs, Stan was thinking.
She's far too good for them. Pearls before swine, that's
what it was.

He knew he was getting a crush on her, quite a bad
one; all the signs were there. He was quick to recognize
them these days. The funny thing was that he could
stand outside himself, and look in on what was happening, but he couldn't do a thing about it.

And she made it much worse by being especially nice
to him. She was nice to anybody who behaved themselves, and worked without fooling around, but she
seemed to have a real soft spot for Stan. He thought it
must be because she knew he was in a foster home and
had no mum or dad.

But last week, first day back after the summer holi-
days, something awful had happened. He'd seen her
driven up to the school gates in a brand-new Volvo and
the man inside had kissed her before she got out. The
crowd by the railings had whistled and hooted; Stan
could have killed them. In the English lesson she was
radiant, more beautiful, somehow, than he could ever

remember, and there was an opal ring on her wedding finger. Stan felt sick with shock and as the day wore on he grew nearly insane with a devouring jealousy. He just couldn't stand it.

Why shouldn't Miss Dobbs get married, the sensible Stan reasoned, looking in on the other, pathetic Stan, eaten up with envy and hurt. Most people marry in the end. Why shouldn't she? What are you, anyway, he asked himself, just an overgrown fourteen-year-old kid. But the real point was that Miss Dobbs had got someone of her own, someone to whom she mattered more than anyone else in the world. That was what he wanted.

But he wasn't running away because his favourite teacher had got herself hitched to a man with a flashy new car, though if he got away from London, and from her, his crush might well cool off a bit. No, it had just worked out that the engagement had come right on top of everything else. It had been all he needed to push him right over the edge.

He'd bought himself a notebook in Woolworths and written 'My Commonplace Book' on the cover because he always did what Miss Dobbs said. Somehow, because he associated it with her and he was never going to see her again, the cheap red exercise book was already precious to him and it was one of the few things he'd brought in the rucksack from Auntie Marjorie's. In the gloom of the shed he opened it at the first page and began to read it through.

'Stan Mellor' he'd written at the top, in small ugly letters because he hated it so much. 'Sid' was even worse. How could anyone have called two brothers 'Sidney' and 'Stanley'? What sort of woman must his mother have been? On the telly nurses who took in abandoned babies called them things like 'Baby Ralph' and 'Baby James'. Any name would have been better than Stan.

Underneath he'd written 'John Keats' because he was Miss Dobbs's favourite poet, then other words he thought were lovely to say, 'Peace', 'Compassion', 'Holy', then 'Epiphany'. Underneath he'd written 'Epiphany' again, in block capitals, and after it 'The Time of the Star'.

It didn't seem to fit with having a husband like Victor but Auntie Marjorie was dead religious. Every Sunday morning she went to the eleven o'clock service in the ugly Victorian church at the end of their road, and the three children went with her. Stan didn't understand what she got out of religion; it certainly didn't make her happy, in fact the more she went to church the more anxious and miserable-looking she seemed to become. Auntie Marjorie worried about most things. She liked fostering kids but it was always 'Don't talk about that when Victor's around', or 'We'd better not mention that to Victor'. Her main hobby seemed to be putting up with her trials, and making sacrifices. Nobody on this earth could have enjoyed those dreary services at St Oswald's but she never missed.

In January, though, he was glad he'd gone because he'd heard something important. It was Epiphany, the time when the Three Kings were supposed to have brought their gifts to the Baby Jesus. Their usual preacher, an old, hunched-up dwarf of a man who looked dead from the neck up, was ill that morning and this very young man had turned up instead. He'd got long blond hair and a fabulous singing voice, and old jeans peeping out from under his cassock.

He'd preached a sermon about the Three Wise Men. It was more like a fairy story than anything else, he'd told them. It could *be* a fairy story for all he cared, it was what it meant now that mattered.

The bit Stan remembered had come right at the end. 'For all of us,' he'd said, 'there comes, one day, the time of the star, just as it came to them. For the Kings it came when they were very old men, but it can happen any time. You could be middle-aged, or a school kid, or quite a young child, but the point is this: whenever it comes you'll definitely *know* about it! Whenever it comes,' he repeated, 'we *know*! Something happens to us, we are electrified! And after that, nothing will ever be quite the same again.'

Nobody else in the church seemed to be listening. Under cover of the pew Elspeth was reading her *Beano* and Auntie Marjorie looked half asleep. Kingsley was busy picking his nose. But Stan heard, and he leaned forward in case he missed anything. He wasn't 'religious' but he knew that this message was for him. It was one of the first things he'd written in his Woolies' notebook, 'The Time of the Star: Epiphany', underlined in felt tip.

He'd been thinking about it for months but not actually *doing* anything; then he smashed Kingsley up, twice in one week. After that he knew his 'time' had come.

Kingsley was always much worse when Victor came home, and now he'd started getting at Elspeth too. Stan wasn't having that. She'd not been at Auntie Marjorie's very long but she meant quite a lot to him already. 'Blood's thicker than water, lovie,' he could hear Mrs Kelly saying it now. And it was true. Elspeth was his flesh-and-blood sister and he'd got to stick up for her.

He didn't even know she existed till about a year ago when one of the social workers turned up and had a long talk with Auntie Marjorie. She'd talked to Stan too. Little Elspeth was their half-sister apparently, his and Sid's, or so they 'believed'.

Fancy not *knowing*. Stan had privately decided that some of these social workers were a bit half-baked. Not so half-baked as his mother though. They said she was still up North, living somewhere near Liverpool. If they were right about Elspeth being his sister she must have had three children by three different men, and she'd not been allowed to keep any of them.

She must be a bit thick then. First, you could stop yourself getting pregnant; second, you didn't have your children taken away unless there was something wrong with you. Social workers didn't go breaking up families unless they had to; Stan knew that much because he kept his ears open, and he'd had social workers fussing round him as long as he could remember.

When he was little he used to think about his mother a lot and sometimes he managed to persuade himself that none of it was her fault. One day, he pretended, he'd get himself to this town she lived in, near Liverpool. He'd just walk through the door and there she'd be, waiting for him in a lovely bright house, with a meal all ready on the table. And a dad would be out at work somewhere, but coming in soon for his tea.

Now, when those dreams came, Stan pushed them back firmly. He understood a lot more, now he was older, and he didn't much want to go looking for his mother. She must be what the social workers called 'an inadequate person'. That meant lazy, or not facing up to her responsibilities, or just plain thick. She couldn't have ever wanted Sid, Stan or Elspeth anyway.

He was in control of his own life now and he wasn't going to let other people mess him around any more. One day, he'd get a really good job, earn money and marry, and have some children, four probably. And someone would always be there, looking after them and loving them. That was his dream now.

He'd liked looking after Elspeth. He didn't quite feel she was his sister, not yet anyhow; a big idea like that took some getting used to. But she certainly needed someone to take care of her, and Stan had discovered he was rather good at that.

She was tiny for a seven-year-old with a pale, almost greenish skin. It made her look as if she ought to be put in the sun for a bit, or back in the oven to brown. Everything frightened her, loud noises, when people shouted, or just the dog yapping, and when Auntie Marjorie gave her a little job she scuttled off to do it like a clockwork mouse. She never spoke unless you spoke to her first, and then it was only Yes or No.

At night she nearly always wet the bed. Stan's heart went out to her over that because it meant she was frightened and unhappy. He'd heard plenty of bed-wetting conversations in the Homes, sometimes it was all they ever seemed to talk about. Auntie Marjorie never said anything, she just stripped the bed and went down to the launderette with the sheets. She was good like that.

Victor wasn't around much. Weeks would go by and they'd not hear a thing from him. It suited Stan. But when he showed up he noticed the smell from the cubby-hole straightaway. He was a very flashy dresser, heavy on the after-shave and the deodorants; he was smooth, Victor was. The Child Welfare people thought he was a travelling rep whose work took him away from home. They weren't supposed to let children go somewhere they weren't happy about, so he must have told them a pack of lies. He could be as nice as pie when he had to be.

Fostering unwanted children was the one thing Auntie Marjorie stood up to him about and they had big rows over it; Stan had heard them. Victor always said the same thing, that he brought good money home and why did she want to saddle herself with snotty-nosed kids, kicking up their row and making the place into a pigsty? She always said the same thing in reply, that the money was nothing to do with it and that she fostered kids because she liked doing it. Someone had to.

'You've got your own child,' Victor had raged on at her, the week Elspeth had arrived. 'What do you want other people's for? Isn't your own son enough for you?'

'*No*,' Auntie Marjorie had snapped back at him, quite viciously for her. And Stan, eavesdropping at the top of the stairs, had smiled to himself. Horrible Kingsley, with his mean little eyes and narrow, shut-in face. He'd got more of his father in him than Auntie Marjorie.

23

Kingsley . . . a name like that had got to be Victor's idea, it was like something out of a spy film. He wasn't at all surprised to hear that Kingsley alone didn't satisfy Auntie Marjorie's mothering instincts, he wouldn't satisfy anyone's.

Elspeth had heard the shouting too, she'd been caught in the kitchen, in the cross-fire. When Victor really raised his voice she always tried to hide behind Auntie Marjorie. That made him even worse.

Stan had given her Fat Cat, his gentle ginger tom, and she really loved him, though she'd renamed him Kitty Wee. It was a daft name for such a large cat and he felt embarrassed when she called 'Kitty Wee, Kitty *Wee*!', out in the street, but he put up with it, for her sake. Kingsley's Alsatian terrified her though and she wouldn't go into the garden when it was there. She said it was 'a wolf'. It took weeks to persuade her to go outside when the dog was around, and when she did she kept right away from it, treading in the narrow flowerbeds of sour London soil to get to the little sandpit at the end.

Whenever she went out to play she always went through the same ritual with horrible Kingsley.

'Kingsley, you won't undo Carl, will you?'

'No.'

'And you won't let him jump up at me, will you?'

'No.'

'You promise, Kingsley, don't you? You really do promise?'

'Look, I've said I won't, haven't I?'

And after that she might go down the garden, but always looking back over her shoulder, just to make sure the dog was still fastened up.

On the day of Fight One Elspeth had plucked up the courage to go out to play. It was a sunny morning and she seemed happy for once; she didn't look over her shoulder to check on the dog. Kingsley had noticed that.

24

The minute she reached the sandpit he let Carl off his chain. The huge dog bounded straight over to her, barking and wagging its tail, rearing up and knocking her over in its exuberance. It was a soft creature and it wouldn't have hurt her but Elspeth wasn't to know that. She dropped her plastic spade and ran for the house, screaming; the dog leaped after her yapping, and showing its teeth.

In the house she became hysterical, in fact, she screamed so violently she made herself sick. Auntie Marjorie had to put her to bed in the end and she was up in the cubby-hole a long time, soothing her down. She was kind to all three of them, and she didn't have favourites.

Out in the garden all Kingsley did was laugh.

Something inside Stan snapped then. Every obscenity he knew came to his lips but mere speech choked him. He was about three times Kingsley's size, so it wasn't much trouble to lift him up and chuck him hard against the rickety shed. Then, as the boy slid to the ground in a heap, he punched him till there was no breath left and blood streamed from his nose and lower lip.

Stan felt better after that. He left him grizzling for his mother, bent up like a hairpin, and slipped out into the alley behind the gardens.

The second time, though, he'd not been so lucky.

He turned to page three of his notebook where he'd copied something out. It was a poem he'd spotted right at the back of Miss Dobbs's new anthology. Stan liked poetry and something in this had caught his attention, so he read it through. It was called 'To My Mother' but Stan knew better. As he looked at it the words leaped out at him from off the page; 'as huge as Asia' he read and then, 'Gin and chicken helpless in her Irish hand', and 'She is a procession no one can follow after/But be like a little dog following a brass band.'

He marvelled over it when he read it again. It was an exact description of Mrs Kelly, the old Irish lady, huge as a small mountain, who'd once looked after him and Sid so tenderly. Where had she gone? Why had she left them on their own like that? They'd never told him. He crossed out 'To My Mother' and instead printed reverently 'To Mrs Kelly'. When he read it again after, up in the bedroom, Stan cried. What happened to people when they died? Perhaps that vicar in jeans could explain to him; he seemed to have his head screwed on.

If Kingsley McCann scraped enough brains together he'd go to a university and study to be a head-shrinker. He seemed to know by instinct what was going on in Stan's mind, and how to hurt him. Or perhaps he'd take after Victor and be a crook, one that always kept his hands clean and never got caught. Stan's bones told him that Victor's money came from thieving. It was in the blood and Kingsley was light-fingered too. More than once Stan had discovered he'd been going through his things.

He must have read the Woolies' notebook.

Kingsley McCann wasn't much younger than Stan but he was childish, always whispering things under his breath, trying to make trouble. He was puny for his age and undersized, so there was no point in raising his fists. Words were his weapon. He chose his moment, at tea, when Victor and Julius were sprawled in the best armchairs, swigging beer out of six-packs, hogging the small gas-fire.

It was only a whisper at first but then, when Stan didn't react, he got louder and louder.

'Mrs Kelly, Mrs Kelly,
Dirty knickers and a big fat belly.'

He repeated it over and over again.

The timing was perfect. Elspeth was still up in the cubby-hole and wouldn't come out; in his brain Stan could still hear those pathetic screams of panic mingled with Kingsley's bleating laugh.

The boy thought he was safe with his dad in the room

but at that moment Stan wasn't afraid of anybody. He advanced on Kingsley and for the second time in twenty-four hours found himself lifting up the other boy under the armpits. The kitchen door, with its blue chipped paint, was behind them. Stan drove his head against the wooden panels three, four, five times. Kingsley's teeth clashed together horribly, the blood poured from his mouth, and he whined pathetically for him to 'leave off'.

Then Victor came up from behind and Stan found himself under the table, his face reduced to a pink jelly by a volley of blows from an iron fist. The man didn't stop kicking him till he cried out in pain. He was a professional.

Auntie Marjorie appeared in the doorway, but she didn't interfere. She was frightened of Victor in this mood. If she tried to stop him he'd turn on her too, and then where would they be? But the minute he'd pushed off, taking Kingsley and Julius with him, she sat Stan down by the gas-fire and bathed his face carefully.

He slid the notebook down a pouch in the side of his rucksack and buckled up the straps. He'd not wanted to leave Elspeth, so soon after they'd found each other, but he'd come back one day and rescue her properly. His face was still very tender, mottled with bruises and broken blood vessels. He stroked at it gingerly and winced.

He'd not known of course that Victor was on the run, though Julius turning up so suddenly should have told him something. He wouldn't have stayed anyway, not now. He'd had as much as he could stand at Auntie Marjorie's and his plans were all worked out. He was determined to find Sid, and Mrs Kelly's family, however long it took. He'd promised himself that. He wanted to be with people who cared about him now, people who wanted him for himself. Mrs Kelly had cared.

Rain poured down on to the shed and dripped

through holes in the roof. The morning was wearing on but it looked as dark as night again. Stan made a face as he pulled his anorak on. Some time to be going, he thought. *Some Star*.

He moved off cautiously on a quiet route he'd memorized, leaving the sprawl of London further and further behind him, heading north. Nobody stopped him. By three o'clock, before the schools were out, he was well on his way, and he could hear and see the M1.

Chapter Three

Stan stood at the roundabout at the point where a slip-road ran off it down to the motorway, under an enormous sign that said 'M1 North'. He wasn't the only person trying to get a lift, several others stood right on the verge, two men and a girl, their thumbs thrust out aggressively, hardly looking at the cars they were trying to stop. Two had pieces of cardboard; one said 'Birmingham' and the other 'Manchester'.

One by one they got picked up. Nobody seemed interested in Stan. Perhaps he looked too scruffy, almost buried in his dark-green anorak with the dripping hood pulled right down to hide his hair. His boots were filthy now and water was running out of them. Perhaps he wasn't casual enough. Perhaps he needed a cardboard notice like the others who'd stood there so defiantly, as if they thought a free ride was their right.

He'd not eaten since eight o'clock and he was hungry. It would have been quite easy to buy food on the way but he'd been nervous about going into shops too near home. There were some biscuits left in his rucksack and he decided to have a few of those. He was swinging it off his back when a large car went past him and turned into the slip-road. It was slowing down and some blurred figures in the back were pointing and jabbing.

Stan's heart kindled with hope. Could they really be stopping for him? He walked slowly towards the champagne-coloured car, an old Mercedes in beautiful condition. Very classy. He was interested in cars. The others had gone off in a Ford Escort, a Mini, and a frozen-food van. It had been worth waiting.

'Where are you bound for, son?'

The passenger window had been opened from the driver's seat by a middle-aged man, and a tanned face and a head of silvery-grey hair was thrust up at him. His eyes were brown. Kind eyes, Stan thought. He was expensively dressed in a checked jacket, fawn trousers and a soft camel-coloured, V-necked sweater. It was warm in the car; sweet string music drifted from a cassette player.

'Liverpool.'

'Hop in then, you picked the right car.'

'Are you going up that far then?'

'Miles beyond there. Up into Scotland. I've got to get these home.' He jerked his head into the back at two small children, a boy and a girl.

'I can drop you off at the M62 interchange. Anyone'll take you into Liverpool from there. Hop in to the back,' he repeated.

Stan hesitated. The car was carpeted in thick rugs, creamy-white.

'My boots are a bit of a mess,' he said. 'I don't want to put mud on your carpets. I could take them off if you like.'

'No, don't bother. Here, put this down, I've finished with it.'

He gave Stan a folded newspaper and he opened it out, spread it on the rug then climbed in, swinging his rucksack up on to his knees. The man leaned past him to check the door was locked then moved the car on to the slip-road. It was a miracle. They were soon gliding along the motorway at a smooth seventy.

'Still at school, are you?' the man said casually.

'No, I've left. In the summer.'

'What are you doing now then?'

'Electrical engineering, through a firm.'

'You're not a Liverpool boy, are you? You're a Londoner, surely?'

Stan started to sweat. He couldn't tell if the man was prying, or just making polite conversation.

'Yes,' he got out. 'My firm's sending me up to do a month's course, at their regional headquarters. You know.'

He hoped this sounded all right and that the man didn't ask him the name of the firm.

'Don't they pay your fares? How come you had to hitch a lift?'

Stan thought rapidly. 'Yes, yes, they do . . . only I . . . some of us,' he stammered.

'I get it, I get it,' the man interrupted. 'This way you can claim the fare and make a bit of money on the side. Well, I don't blame you.'

He seemed satisfied for the moment and he turned the music up; then he lit a cigarette. Stan sat there, nervous and silent, staring at his muddy boots, hugging the rucksack.

The children looked about ten and eight and they were huddling away from Stan suspiciously, leaving a great strip of seat between him and them. The back of the car was a litter of comics and toffee papers, there were several packets of sweets and a big slab of chocolate, unopened. Stan's mouth began to water now. He'd got real hunger pains.

They were quite skimpily dressed, an odd contrast with the rainy outside. The hot spell had ended that morning in thunder followed by a straight downpour. Rain was hurtling down on the top of the car from a sky the colour of tin. They wore sandals on bare feet, and shorts and T-shirts in smart, contrasting colours. Their skin was a deep, even brown, their hair bleached white. Both of them stared coldly at Stan as if he was some monster that had crept out of a bog.

'You smell!' the girl said suddenly, and dissolved into giggles. The boy laughed too, though nervously.

'Leave it you two, just leave it, or I'll knock your bloody heads together,' the man said viciously, but his voice sounded weary, as if he'd said all this before. Stan wondered where the mother was.

'I'm sorry,' he said. 'Take no notice of them. They're just kids.'

'It's OK,' Stan muttered in an embarrassed mumble. He wasn't used to having his feelings considered much, or to people saying they were sorry. Things had never been very personal in his world, it was more a case of numbers, of being shunted about and fitted into spaces by people you didn't often see. It was a done-to life.

The girl was right anyway, he did smell because he was beginning to sweat horribly inside the waterproof anorak. The warm fug inside the car was getting unbearable and hunger was making him light-headed. Stan thought he might actually pass out if he couldn't get a bit cooler so he pushed his hood back and pulled off the knitted hat. At once his curls sprang from captivity. The children stared at them and giggled openly.

They were just a couple of thick rich kids Stan decided, as he listened to their prattle, kids that had been obviously spoilt rotten by people with more money than sense. They'd been in the South of France all summer and now they were going back to their mother in Scotland. They said nothing else to him but when the excitement of his arrival had faded they started to fight.

Everything displeased them. They didn't like the comics or the sweets and they both wanted to sit near the window. First they said their father was going too fast, then too slow. Then the girl wanted to wind the window down and the boy tried to wind it up again. Then they both grizzled at the man till he took off the tape of violin music and put some pop music on instead.

Stan didn't envy them. Neither of them seemed the

least bit happy and they looked how they acted, permanently discontented, with the mean, grabbing look of Kingsley McCann. Their parents must be separated, or divorced. They weren't free to do what they wanted, like him; they were pushed around everywhere and there was a lot more of that coming to them. It was a done-to life for them too, for all their money. He rather pitied them.

In the end they opened the chocolate and immediately starting squabbling about sharing it out.

'Give – what's your name?'

'Bob, Bob Kelly.'

'Well, give Bob some, for God's sake,' the man said irritably. After a minute the girl pushed one mingy square at him, with a resentful stare.

'No thanks,' Stan said, famished as he was. He could do without that.

His eyes ran aimlessly over the newspaper spread out under his boots. The man must have read it over his lunch because it was today's, the early evening edition of a London daily. Suddenly his stomach tightened into a hard, painful knot, a shock wave hit him and his ears started to sing. The main headline was in gigantic letters 'Massive North London Drugs Seizure – Man Held' and underneath in smaller type 'Missing Boy Connection'. Then there were three photographs in a line. One of them was his.

The girl, Amanda, was grizzling for her father to stop so she could go to the lavatory.

'OK, OK, we'll have ten minutes here and you can both go and run round for a bit.'

The Mercedes turned off into a service area and headed for a space marked 'Cars Only'. Stan saw three empty police cars lined up on the slope of the hard shoulder.

The car-park was very crowded and they had to go

right on the edge of it, several rows away from lavatories, shops and cafés. The children were out in a couple of seconds, running towards the shops, dodging the moving cars. The father yelled at them to take care, but they acted deaf.

'Do you want a breather, Bob?' he said kindly. 'Come on, I'll buy you a cup of coffee, or a beer?'

'No thanks,' Stan said, 'I'll just wait here. Don't suppose you'll be all that long, will you?'

'Only five minutes or so. Just as you like.'

Stan stared after him, following the large silvery head and the broad checked shoulders above the rows of cars. He watched him get to the sweetshop and stand outside, looking around for his children. As he peered through the glass doors a policeman came out of the café area and went up to him.

After a minute's talk they both turned round and looked in the direction of the Mercedes. The driver said something to the policeman who nodded and pointed at the car and then ran his hands over his head, fanning them out. He was describing Stan's hair.

The boy paused only to grab the newspaper and shove it into a ball down the pouch of his rucksack. Then he opened the door and leaped out.

In the time it took the two men to walk out to the car Stan had got to the lorry-park. He was sliding in and out of the huge rows, the truck sides towering darkly over him, ending in slits of light, like the overgrown walls of some nightmare city. The combined smells of rubber, oil and sweat made his empty stomach crease and turn over. He retched drily and his head swam with a sickly pain. After a minute or so he crept to the edge of the lorries and peered out over the car-park.

They were still standing by the Mercedes and the driver was pointing to the open rear door. The police officer stared round vaguely and scratched his head, then looked down at his notebook. Then two more came running up, out of the café area. They ignored the car-driver but started to jabber at the policeman, moving away as they talked, pointing down the motorway with their ballpoint pens.

Stan had spotted the lavatories of the transport café at the other end of the lorry-park. The building was on its own, a walk away from the main complex. He reckoned they might not look for him there, at least not yet. So he chose his moment then belted across the tarred path, shouldering the door open. A large man came out doing up the flies of his boiler-suit and collided with him.

'Watch it, mate!' a fat voice bellowed, and the lorry-driver stared at him irritably. Stan had tripped over the man's boots in the doorway and now he went flying, landing by the urinals on all fours. His rucksack skidded away from him and landed underneath the hot-air machine.

'Fer *Gawd's sake!*' the man yelled, turning round and rubbing his shin.

Suddenly losing his nerve, Stan left the rucksack where it was and shut himself in one of the cubicles. He leaned back against the door, panting painfully. How long would it take them to get this far?

The lady at the café had always dreamed of 'helping the police with their inquiries' and now she was. She could hardly wait till they got to her table. Yes, she told them, she *had* seen somebody thumbing a lift, on the other side of the motorway, just as she'd driven in. It was illegal, wasn't it? She'd been warning her two boys here not to copy. Yes, he was definitely wearing some kind of anorak and it could well have been green. He'd got a rucksack, and curly hair – very blond. She'd especially noticed it. And he'd got a lift in a red car, rather a sporty model, she thought.

The police went back to the car-park, told Stan's lift they'd made a mistake, and apologized. Minutes later they were roaring up the motorway at ninety, sure they were on to something. You couldn't tell the public too much, in a case like this.

It was some considerable time before they found and flagged down the red Ford Capri and the boy in the anorak wasn't too pleased to be interrogated about his role in a drugs swoop by two policemen. He was rather a superior young man, a final-year English student at Lancaster University, and he was going back early to star in a play. His name was Rodney du Cane and he was tall, heavily built and handsome, with clusters of thick blond curls.

Miles back, in the lavatory cubicle, Stan sat tight.

Chapter Four

He didn't move out of it for an hour, but sat there, on the lid of the lavatory seat, analysing the noises. Every time the main door opened his heart lurched. Now and then somebody would go into one of the cubicles and when the footsteps approached Stan braced himself. He was waiting for a pair of well-shined black shoes to appear in the gap under the door, and for someone to start hammering on it.

But nobody did. Shadows came and went, cisterns flushed and filled up again, people ran taps and left them dripping. Apart from the faint hum of the motorway it was very quiet. Once somebody stayed a long time by the hot-air machine drying his hands and Stan got nervous. He could see a shadow under the door.

But whoever it was went off in the end. Stan heard the small change clinking in his pocket, and he was whistling.

When he was certain there was no one outside his door he unlocked it and came out. The rucksack was just where he'd left it, under the hand-dryer. He grabbed it and shut himself in the cubicle again.

The building faced on to a tarmacked road. Behind was a high barbed-wire fence, and beyond that were fields. Stan was in luck. Although there was the usual small ventilation window set into the glass, the whole of the window opened as well. He climbed up and flung the small rucksack through, over the fence, then he squeezed out on to the narrow ledge and jumped after it. He cleared the barbed-wire easily and hit the ground hard, then rolled several feet down a steep bank into a field that bristled with sharp stalks.

The daylight was going. He spotted his rucksack a few feet away, grabbed it then ran into the cover of a huge cutting-machine that had been left on the edge of the stubble, half-way down the field. The orange glow of the motorway buildings was away up behind him, in front the darkening field spread out and a scattering of lights twinkled at the edge of it. Stan hoped it was a village, he must find some food soon.

First though there was the newspaper. He opened the pouch and undid the crumpled ball, smoothing it out over the spiky grass. In another of the pouches he'd put a small torch; he switched it on and ran the narrow beam over the newsprint.

The other photographs were of Victor and Julius. Stan read:

> Scotland Yard claimed last night to have seized drugs in a North London raid worth a record amount on the streets. Thirty-seven-year-old Victor McCann, whom the police have wanted for questioning for some considerable time, was arrested in the incident and is expected to appear in court later today. The swoop came after a prolonged investigation into a series of drugs rackets nationwide. Police also want to interview a man who calls himself Julius Lodge, believed to be working with McCann. They warn that Lodge could be dangerous and should not be approached.

Stan stared hard at the picture of Julius. 'Calls himself' the news story said. That fitted. It surely couldn't be anyone's real name? The man had probably copied it from one of those crime thrillers he read whenever he came to see Victor. There was a whole stack of them in Auntie Marjorie's front room.

He looked like a rat, his whole face growing to a point.

Sharpish nose, slit mouth, close-set eyes. He'd got a whiskery moustache with straggly sideburns that he stroked nervously when he talked, and he chewed gum all the time, the small mouth half open so that you could see his tongue, pushing the stuff round his teeth.

He wasn't smart-looking like Victor so he couldn't be one of the men up front. People like Julius Lodge kept in the shadows, doing the dirty, sneaky jobs. Last week he'd had the same clothes on every day; jeans, and a red polo-necked jersey, and a black leather jacket. It was grey with dandruff and cigarette ash. They looked the same clothes in this photo.

Something in the face frightened Stan. He wasn't at all surprised to discover, reading down the report, that Julius Lodge had once served a long prison sentence for robbery with violence. Victor wasn't much better. His photo was on the front page because he'd injured a policeman. He'd fired several shots as he tried to get away and now a young detective lay critically ill in hospital with a bullet in his stomach.

Stan shuddered, remembering the noise in the night, the noise he'd thought was a car backfiring. Whether the policeman lived or died, Victor McCann would be in prison for years. Someone in the Child Welfare department would have a red face now, for not doing their homework properly. He wouldn't be sent back to Auntie Marjorie's, not even if they caught him. Not that they would catch him.

Now he understood why there'd been so many policemen along the motorway. In London missing boys were kids' stuff, they'd never have sent all those men out just to look for Stan Mellor. They only wanted him because of what he could tell them. Because of Victor McCann and Julius Lodge. Because he'd gone missing the same night as the shoot-out. Because a policeman might die. They didn't want him for himself.

He folded the paper up small and pushed it back into

the pouch, then he felt down the side of the rucksack for the plastic bag of banknotes he'd pushed to the bottom. It wasn't there, neither was the other bank bag that had contained three pounds in silver. Stan couldn't believe it.

He tipped everything out and started to go through it feverishly. There wasn't much, a pair of jeans and a sweater rolled up round two T-shirts, some underpants and a few pairs of socks. There was a sponge-bag with washing things in it, the Woolworth's notebook and a couple of ballpoint pens.

He found three biscuits too but he couldn't eat them, his mouth had gone very dry and hard. While he was hiding in the lavatory someone had stayed a long time by the hand-dryer, fiddling about. That was where his rucksack had ended up. Whoever it was had gone through it and taken his money, all twenty-three pounds of it. No wonder he'd gone off whistling.

You needed cash for a journey and Stan had been saving up for a long time. You had to pay your way and survive, you had to eat. He was crossing over to Ireland so he'd needed the money for a ferry ticket. But if he was going to last out now he'd have to cadge off people. Or steal.

For a few minutes he felt numb. Then he stuffed everything back into the rucksack, stood up, and swung it on his back. Desperately he shone the torch over the grass. His heart flipped over when he spotted a small plastic bag at the edge of the small circle of light, but when his fingers closed on it, and he brought it up close to his face, Stan saw that it did not contain his money but a whitish powder, slightly granular, like fine washing-soda.

The bag was made of very thick polythene, heat-sealed at the edges. Stan weighed it in his hand. He judged it contained several ounces. This was the squishy package he'd seen Victor hide by his bed, last night. It must have been meant for Kingsley's bag, not his. Stan remembered now, how he'd looked helplessly from bed to bed. They both had identical grey canvas rucksacks that they used for school. Auntie Marjorie had got them from the Army Surplus shop. Victor must have meant to come back for this packet, or else he'd tipped off Julius about it.

Stan stared at the white powder and a numbness crept through him. What was it? Cocaine? Heroin? He didn't know what those things looked like. Some of the people at their school had been caught with drugs and the Head had called a special meeting for the parents. Auntie Marjorie had told them all about it. 'If you think your child won't be offered drugs in the next year or so,' he'd said, 'then I'm afraid you're living in a fantasy world.' And she'd issued all kinds of warnings to him and Kingsley, she'd been quite nasty for her. *Drugs*. It was a laugh when you thought of Victor.

He'd never wanted to get into that anyway; part of it was that advert on the telly. 'I can handle it,' the boy kept saying, but you could tell he was kidding himself. He looked like Gary Whittaker in 4B . . . the one who sniffed glue, red-eyed and blotchy, and half asleep all the time.

It was dead easy to get hold of drugs in London. When he got married Stan was planning to live in the country where the drug-pushers and weirdos couldn't get at his children. It was part of the plan he had for his life.

He stuffed the packet right down to the bottom of the rucksack. Somehow he didn't even like touching it. People did anything for drugs, they even killed for them. And if that young police officer died it'd be another drugs murder.

How much was this bit of the haul worth, he wondered, shouldering the rucksack. Hundreds probably, perhaps thousands. Drugs were big money, he knew that much. It wasn't a fat lot of use to him though, he couldn't eat it.

All he wanted was the money he'd saved for running away and that must be whizzing up the motorway now, in some creep's back pocket.

Stan had never stolen anything in his life, but when it came to it he found it quite easy. A church clock was striking as he got to the lights. It was hardly a village, just a straggle of houses along a lane. He could hear traffic faintly, half a mile behind him, on the road that came off the motorway just before the service area.

He was in luck. There was only one shop in the place, a small tatty-looking supermarket called Mike's. The sign on the door said 'Friday: Late Night Shopping till 8 p.m.'. And it was Friday, and still open. Stan pushed at the door and went in.

The shop was empty and unnervingly quiet. There was nobody around except a young girl at the check-out. She'd already put her coat on and she looked at Stan resentfully.

'You'll have to be quick, we're closing.'

Stan nodded and walked to the back of the shop, his head and neck prickling with nerves. The shop was a pigsty. Untidy heaps of tins and packets, too higgledy-piggledy to be called displays, were dumped all over the place, blocking the aisles. It was difficult to move without knocking things over and there were cartons everywhere, half-emptied or flattened for the refuse lorry, or just flung about in corners.

The jumble gave him good cover though. He could have taken loads of stuff if he'd had an empty bag, and the nerve. But when it came to the crunch and he actually had to put his hand out and take the food off the shelf, he went icy-cold. This was stealing. If she spotted him it would be all over, and everything would be a thousand times worse than before.

But Stan reasoned this way, a thief had stolen his money so he'd had nothing to eat for the whole day. It wasn't how he'd planned it but it wasn't his fault. Before he got another lift he'd write down what he'd taken in his notebook, and the name of the shop. Perhaps one day he'd be able to send the money back.

Outside a car hooted smartly. The check-out girl was buttoning her coat and she peered down the aisles, looking for Stan.

'Get a move on, can't you? I told you, we're closing.'

He grabbed a packet of sausage rolls and a pork pie, two apples on a cardboard tray and a carton of milk, and pushed them all down into the rucksack. As he walked slowly up to the till he turned sideways and slipped a chocolate bar into his pocket. At the check-out there was the usual rack of sweets. He took a Mars bar and pushed it at the girl with a twenty-pence he'd found in the back pocket of his jeans, when he was hiding in the lavatories.

She looked at it disbelievingly. 'Fer Gawd's sake, is that all yer wanted?'

Stan nodded.

'Well, that's not enough, they've gone up.' She pointed behind her to a price list.

Stan didn't budge. 'I . . . I wanted quite a few things, Miss,' he said, 'but I came out without my money.'

She looked at him curiously, interested in spite of herself. He was quite good-looking, and she liked being called 'Miss'.

'Where you from then?'

'Over Rushfield way.' He remembered the name from the motorway.

'What you doin' here then?'

'Oh, just visiting somebody, y'know.' He smiled at her and pushed the Mars bar back at her. Outside the car hooted again.

The girl was filled with the charitable glow of Friday night. She was going drinking with her boyfriend.

'Oh, go on then, have it. Never say I don't give you nothing. Get out of me sight.' And she actually grinned at him. This was being friendly.

'Thanks,' Stan said. He pushed his way out of the shop as she switched all the lights off, thankful for the sudden darkness, hoping she wouldn't look at his bulging rucksack with the things he'd stolen, hidden under the clothes.

He went back to the field and sat by the cutting-machine, and in a few minutes had eaten everything except one of the apples and the Mars bar. Then he got out his notebook and wrote 'Mike's Minimart, near Rushfield, Northants.'. He was putting the notebook away when he suddenly reopened it and added, 'The girl definitely fancied me. She let me have a Mars for 20p.'

And he smiled to himself in the darkness. He was still free and he'd survived so far. The next thing was to get a lift up to Liverpool.

Chapter Five

Something was on fire in the middle of the motorway buildings. As he got back over the fence, he could see a yellowy glare and smell smoke. A fire-engine had arrived and its lights flashed into the dark, illuminating the circle of faces that stood round. Some kind of long truck was slewed across the slope that led down to the road. A policeman was dealing with a long back-up of cars and lorries, squeezing them slowly through the gap that was left open.

He'd been going to walk straight down the slip-road and thumb a lift near the bottom, but suddenly he felt brave. The darkness and the crowd, the confusion round the burning engine, gave him the courage to creep up and join the people that were watching. Nobody even looked at him. The solitary policeman was cursing the slow drivers under his breath. He'd been off duty, going home to Rushfield, when this lot happened.

Stan looked round. The truck-driver was standing with one of the firemen doing a lot of explaining with his hands, imitating a huge lorry going out of control, with smoke pouring from the bonnet. The fireman, still at work on the dying blaze, was nodding and nodding, but not really listening. The onlookers were mainly men, with a few children who'd dragged their dads over to have a look; their clothes were colourless, the whole scene shadowy apart from the sickly motorway glare. Then Stan felt eyes on him.

On the other side of the truck somebody in the crowd was staring straight at him. Stan himself looked out on to darkness but his own face was lit up in flashes by the fire-engine. He stepped back but as he did so whoever it was began to skirt round the edge of the crowd, in his direction.

There was a small light fixed to a wall over a cigarette machine; as the person slipped past it Stan saw a face in a quick square of brightness. Terror clawed him and he started to run away, away from that face with its nose, mouth and tiny eyes, all somehow growing to a point, the interminable twisting and nibbling of face and whiskers.

Ratface.

Julius.

How could he be here?

Stan circled the crowd and hopped across a space between two cars that were crawling past the policeman. Then he glanced back. *Julius.* He'd reached the fire-engine now. Stan saw his face splashed for a second with blue light. Then darkness obliterated him again.

The boy went into the shop that sold sweets and cigarettes, where the Mercedes driver had looked in for his children. The long aisle was empty and Stan walked right up to the end where there was a tall display of magazines and got behind it, keeping one eye on the door. Then a red blodge appeared behind the glass pane. Julius was pushing the door open.

Stan crouched down and peered through the metal struts of the display rack. Ratface had seen him, but he wasn't hurrying. A couple of men had just come in and were buying cigarettes. Julius had to be careful, like Stan. He couldn't afford to draw attention to himself. In spite of the big round glasses he was wearing, and the different way he'd combed his hair, he still looked like that photograph put out by the police.

If he was to get Stan it would have to be a quick, silent
ob.

He started to walk slowly down the aisle towards the
magazine rack. Stan slipped round the other side and
went towards the till, hidden from Julius by the central
displays of sweets and comics. At the door he collided
with somebody coming in, and he had to wait for a
second. He could see Julius reflected in the glass panel,
whipping round to look for him. Outside again he
started to walk more quickly.

He turned left and crossed the bridge that spanned
the motorway. Below him the traffic hurtled past, a dark
muffled roar of winking lights. He'd never been in a
place like this before, it was thrilling. In different circum-
stances he'd have stopped right in the middle to feel the
deep pulse of excitement as the train of machines flew
past, so close to the soles of his boots. All that power,
and Stan on top of it. Like God.

But Julius was running now. At the end of the bridge
there were two lavatory entrances. Stan opened the
men's, went inside and leaned against the door, panting.
Then he had to move over to let someone come out. As
the man disappeared Julius entered and went straight
to the washbasins, looking under the doors of the shut
cubicles. Stan darted through the main door again and
went back over the bridge. There was a staircase at the
end, and a sign pointing up to a self-service café. He
started to climb the stairs at a run.

Inside the cafeteria there was a long queue of people
with trays, shuffling past the plastic shelves of food. He
could tag on to them, Julius wouldn't approach him
there. Then he noticed a row of little booths with high-
backed seats where you could eat privately. It was a no-
smoking area with nobody in it. Stan bypassed the queue
and went to sit down, took a few deep breaths and
swung the rucksack off his shoulders, so he could lean
back for a minute.

47

Julius was after the drugs, not him. If he handed the packet over the man'd clear off most likely, and that would be the end of it. Stan would be free to get himself to Ireland, like he'd always planned. Having Julius Lodge on his back, a man whose photo was all over the papers, was the last thing he wanted at the moment. He was a boy on the run.

But when he thought about giving Ratface the packet something inside him hardened. The people he and Victor worked for were probably millionaires, 'barons' they were called, he'd picked that up from the telly. Men like that would stop at nothing to get what they wanted, they were killers.

Stan didn't intend to give them any help, so he was keeping this little bag until he'd shaken Julius off; in fact he could keep it till he found Sid and tell him the whole story. Joe Kelly would know what to do with it, they could ask him.

Victor and Julius were cheats anyhow, nobody knew about this bit of the haul except them. They'd obviously planned to make a bit of private money on the side. Now it was in Stan's rucksack, hidden by three pairs of underpants. In a different situation he would have laughed out loud.

From where he was sitting he couldn't see the main door, it was cut off from him by a low wall. Every time someone edged past with a tray his heart turned over. He swivelled round on his seat and looked out over the motorway. On his left was the illuminated bridge he'd crossed and recrossed. Behind frosted glass blurred figures were walking to and fro.

One looked like Julius. The lower half of the figure was a black and red blodge but through the clear upper glass Stan saw a flash of spectacles and sleeked-back sandy hair. It was crossing over quickly to the south-bound side.

He stood up, swung the rucksack back on, and made

for the door. But he'd made a mistake about the man in the glass; Julius was behind him, getting up leisurely from a corner seat. He'd been waiting a good ten minutes for the boy to make a move. Now their eyes met.

Back outside Stan made his second mistake; he went for the darkness, running across the car- and lorry-parks, out of the light, climbing the high fence, tearing his hands on rusty barbed-wire. Soon he was back in the field at the bottom of the bank, running anywhere in his panic, not thinking straight.

Julius was over the fence like a cat, and breathing more easily. This was child's play. The dark chase was for him, he was made for it, not too tall and very lightly built. The boy was heavier, weighed down by the bag on his back and the flapping, unzipped anorak.

Stan saw him silhouetted on the rim of the field with the motorway glare behind him, and he watched as he picked something up out of the grass, a stick, or a bar of some kind. People chucked all kinds of rubbish over the fence in places like this. It looked like a piece of exhaust pipe. He wouldn't stand much of a chance if Julius clubbed him over the head with it.

He cowered away into the shadow of the cutting-machine then looked up fearfully. The field ended at the slip-road and sloped sharply down from it, forming a high bank. Julius had lost him for a minute but he was making his way towards the cutter. Stan could hear the faint crunch of his shoes on the brittle grass. Down in the field the high bank had reduced the car noises to a low hum.

'You've put me to a lot of trouble, mate, do you know that?' The voice was a whine, slithery and thin like its owner. 'I've driven nearly two hundred miles up and down this bloody motorway, looking for bloody you, wasting my time, and I'm not wasting any more. Get it? I said, *Get it*?'

Silence. He was waiting for the boy to react. The

slightest intake of breath, a cough, the least movement would be enough to pinpoint him in the dark field. But Stan was wary. His only option was to get away from this enclosed space and go for the open again, under the lights. Julius wouldn't approach him in public. Here, in the shadows, he could smash his head to a pulp with that lump of iron and nobody would be any the wiser.

He was big and brawny, and considerably stronger than Julius Lodge, but if it came to a fight he'd be at a disadvantage with the rucksack weighing him down, and he wasn't dumping that. He could manage without his clothes and stuff, and he'd got no money to lose, but he wasn't letting Ratface get his hands on the plastic bag. It was against all sense, all reason, all chance of escape, but Stan was absolutely determined not to let it go.

He left Julius talking to himself in the middle of the field and began crawling backwards on his belly, away from the machine. It was his only chance. He reached the bank and started to climb up it again, in the direction of the motorway. As he cleared the top and threw himself over the fence Julius saw him, black against the lights, but by the time he'd got over Stan was already on the slip-road and half-way down. The crawling queue of cars and lorries stretched right back up the slope and the policeman was still gloomily signalling traffic past the burnt-out truck.

He ran straight along the hard shoulder on to the motorway itself, but Julius was only ten yards behind him now with the rusty lump of exhaust pipe still in his hand. A huge blue lorry was pulling out into the slow lane but the driver had to jam his brakes on suddenly as something came up behind him too quickly, filling the gap in the traffic.

The truck was still moving but Stan leapt at the cab door, grabbing for the handle. He wrenched it downwards and the door swung open and hit him, sending him sprawling on to the tarmac. He got back on his feet, ran after the truck and lunged up again towards the open door, grasping at a thick bright bar that was screwed on the side. Then with one almighty heave he flung himself bodily into the driving cabin. The heavy door swung behind him as the wheels moved forwards, and chunked into place.

'For Christ's *sake*! You stupid *bastard*!' the driver yelled, but he was too far out into the stream of traffic to pull over again. Some fool behind him was going too fast and would have rammed him from the back.

'Please . . .' Stan moaned. 'Oh *please* . . . somebody's after me.' There was blood all over his hands from the barbed-wire and blood on his face where the cab door had swung and smashed into him. The last crazy run had torn at his stomach and his mouth was bitter with the salt taste of blood. He leaned forward and thrust his head between his knees while the world swam and churned on round him.

In dumb amazement the lorry-driver forged on through the night.

Chapter Six

He was called Jack Brierley and he drove lorries for a road haulage firm. 'Gibbs Transport, Warrington and St Helens' was painted along the side of the truck in yellow letters. He kept looking from the road ahead to the boy at his side but Stan was out cold, on the floor of the cabin. He'd fallen forward heavily, only seconds after his mad leap away from Julius, scraping his face on the facia of the cab and its battery of switches and sharp knobs, drawing more blood. Now he lay in a heap on the floor, all hunched up and puffy like a fat green caterpillar, the skin of the anorak bloated with air. Sweat glistened greenly on his skin which was thinly ribboned with blood, hardly a pulse showing.

After a mile or so the traffic thinned and strung itself out again; the faster vehicles gathered speed quickly and were swallowed up in the dark. As soon as it was safe Jack Brierley pulled over on to the hard shoulder and set his hazard-warning lights flashing. First he went to the rear of the truck to check his load; as he did so a black Mini pulled over behind him, a couple of hundred yards away. After a minute he swung himself up into the cabin, switched the light on, and took a long look at the boy.

Stan opened his eyes and saw something like an illuminated seaside pier with a big face superimposed on it. The strings of winking lights were drops of rain on the truck windows, each water bead caught and enlarged by the rushing headlamps. The big ugly face staring down at him was Jack Brierley's.

The passenger seat had been tipped back slightly now and he was half sitting, half lying. His anorak had been peeled off and rolled in a neat bundle with his rucksack on top of it. They were stowed on the cabin floor by his feet. His hands and forehead throbbed and there was an antiseptic smell creeping over him, bringing the muzzy feeling back again.

Jack snapped the lid back on to his first-aid box and stuffed the bloody cotton wool into a paper rubbish bag clipped underneath the dashboard. He was a tidy man. His large brown eyes were fixed on Stan, but neither of them spoke.

For an opener he offered the boy his lunch-box, thick sandwiches made of fresh brown bread, tomatoes and home-made cake.

'No thanks. I couldn't eat anything. I feel sick.'

'All right, get this down you then.'

He gave Stan something from out of a flask and added a dash from a brown medicine bottle.

'It's rum, this. I don't drink myself. But the wife always makes me carry it, for emergencies like.'

Stan hesitated. He felt too queasy to keep much down.

'Come on, mate, it'll settle you a bit. Drink it off.' And the man watched him carefully.

He emptied the cup in one gulp; it was very sweet coffee, edged with rum. It seemed to plunge slowly down into his heaving stomach and flatten it out slightly.

'Is that better at all?'

Stan nodded.

'OK. Put your belt on, we can't stay here.'

He leaned over and clipped the broad strap into position for Stan, then swung the truck out into the traffic. Four cars back there was a black Mini, silvered with rain-drops. The two shiny discs that gleamed just above the steering-wheel were spectacles.

Jack Brierley had been taken off his guard. He'd been going quietly along, minding his own business and looking forward to a couple of days at home with Chris and the twins, when this had happened. A big curly-headed lad, scared out of his life and covered with blood, had flung himself up into the cabin as he was coming out of Rushfield Services, saying there was somebody chasing him. Then he'd passed out, banging his head on the dashboard. Jack had cleaned him up with cotton wool but it still looked quite nasty. He suspected there was nobody after him. Lads like this would do all sorts to get a lift; there wasn't much money around these days to get yourself round the country on buses, let alone trains. The service stations were full of hitch-hikers in the same boat and they often confided in him.

He stole another glance at Stan. He was a big chap, but surely not very old. It was hard to tell really. His face was filthy after hours on the road, his curls a matted tangle, straggled over his forehead. He was staring ahead rigidly.

Jack took in the large, straight nose, the firm chin, the mouth too tightly pressed. The boy's eyes were full of tears and he was shaking slightly. The lorry-driver knew that look very well, he'd got two teenage sons of his own.

He checked behind in his wing mirror. It was clear enough now, with the traffic well spaced out. Nothing much behind except that Mini way back in the slow lane, still going steadily. It was time to sort things out.

'All right, mate, let's know what happened. What's your name?'

'Bob Kelly.'

'And where've you come from? The South? London?'

'London.'

'And where are you making for?'

'Liverpool.'

'Got relations up there, have you?'

'My mother. She used to live there.'

It was true, more or less. She'd lived somewhere near Liverpool anyhow, according to the social workers.

'Well, I'm going to Warrington, it's where I live and it's pretty close. No problem getting a lift into Liverpool from there. Or there's a train. Heard of Warrington, have you? Warrington New Town? They invested millions in it.'

Warrington. Out of the seas of remembrance Stan plucked the name. Memories. The endless wash of people talking boringly about who he was, and about who Sid was. Auntie Marjorie and Mrs Kelly and before them the matron of a Home. And all the social workers. Warrington and Chorley Street and an older sister called Auntie Dawn.

'Have you heard of it?' Jack repeated.

'Yes. My mother's family used to live there I think, way back.'

'Ever been there yourself?'

'I suppose I must have. Can't remember really.' And Stan stared at his boots, uninterested, neutral.

'And who did you say was after you? Your dad? Your stepfather?'

Stan hadn't said, and he didn't now. He just pulled his mouth about and concentrated on his boots, hoping the man would stop probing.

'Are you trying to get back to your mam? Is that it? They've been fighting over you, have they?'

In the dim cabin the boy seemed to nod in agreement. Jack Brierley was piecing something together rapidly, he liked a good TV play as much as his wife, Chris; they both enjoyed a drama. 'Tug of love' child this boy could have been and the selfish buggers were still at it. Poor little sod.

It was quiet in the cabin. The lorry plunged on through the rainy dark, a steady fifty-five, keeping to the slow lane, with the stolen Mini with Julius Lodge at the wheel a measured quarter-mile behind. Jack Brierley stroked the side of his face with his fingers, something he always did when thinking hard. Stan drowsed beside him, cocooned in warmth and silence and, for the moment, safety, catching, as they floated up to him in fragments, snatches of the lorry-driver's peaceful soliloquy.

'I've got two boys, Stuart and Barry, twins. About your age I should think. How old are you?'

'Sixteen.'

'Ah, you're a bit older then, fourteen mine are. The wife works, she's a school secretary. The money's useful and it's something to do while I'm away, me being on this lark and everything. I get good breaks of course. I've got the next two days off as a matter of fact. We all enjoy that.'

'What do you do?' Stan asked, for something to say.

'Oh, plenty. I like DIY, that sort of thing. Chris has always got the jobs lined up for me. I enjoy it. Then there's the twins, mad on sport they are. They watch everything. I'm taking them to watch Liverpool tomorrow.'

Stan's father, Mellor, might have been anyone. He knew nothing about him at all, apart from his name. He might have been a policeman, or someone off Liverpool docks. Or a long-distance lorry-driver like this, with a kindly, ugly face. He could see it all, the house pin-bright, mother Chris in a pinafore cutting the sandwiches, the twins fresh-faced and noisy. Big Jack Brierley coming in off the lorry, loving them all.

He thought, such a man could have been my father.

But he was nodding off. He'd let his anorak fall to the floor and he was now clutching the rucksack on his knees with a kind of passion that did not seem to grow less, even in sleep. The lorry-driver glanced at it and wondered if Stan had really told him the truth. Then he shrugged. *Lads*. He was sixteen so he could do what he wanted. He looked a nice boy though, and somehow not quite ready to make his own way in life. He wouldn't want either of the twins to be wandering about in motorway service areas, getting lifts, let alone half killing themselves by jumping on to moving lorries.

He'd skimped on sleep so that he could wind up the job in record time, and now he felt drowsy. He was ahead of schedule and there was more than enough time for a few hours' kip. Eighty miles from Warrington he pulled off the road into a big service area and drove into the lorry-park, steering the truck right on to the edge, under some trees. Before getting comfortable he checked round the back, and tried Stan's door to make sure it was still locked. Then he climbed back into his own seat, locked himself in, and tipped the seat back. Within two minutes he was asleep and snoring loudly.

There was no way Julius could penetrate the lorry. Seconds after Jack Brierley had switched his engine off the Mini had stopped too, a few dozen yards away in the car-park. The man snaked his way in and out of the rows of vehicles then plunged into the bigger shadows made by the lorries, always seeking the darkness, away from the pale orange lights.

The long blue truck was the firm's very latest. The triple bolts and clasps of the rear doors gleamed on and off in the headlamps as cars swung past. Silently, under cover of the trees, Julius gripped the bar that had saved Stan and pulled himself up. In the cabin he saw a fat middle-aged man, snoring hugely, his mouth wide open. The boy slept too with the rucksack clutched on his knees.

Julius prowled round and round the cabin like a hungry bear, but it was shut against him, all the windows rolled up and the doors fast. A gun would have shattered them, two or three shots would be enough, and in the confusion he could leap in, grab what he wanted and make off.

But he took his hand away from the pistol that was strapped to his vest underneath the red jersey and thrust it back viciously into his pocket. There might be police around and people would hear, and come running. He'd have to wait till he could corner the boy on his own.

He took a last look at Stan's rucksack. Under his hard gaze the canvas melted away and deep inside the precious package glowed and burned. The man ached for it and his fingers twitched. But he slipped away finally, back to the black Mini, and sat there waiting for signs of life from the lorry, fighting back the waves of sleep that nudged and slapped at him, with a threat of drowning.

Hours later, when he woke up, Gibbs's new truck had vanished.

Chapter Seven

Twenty-past eight and the long blue lorry was stuck in a
traffic jam that looked solid, all the way into Warrington
town centre. The road ahead widened out into a bridge
that arched over a dirty-looking river but nothing at all
was moving. Jack Brierley clicked his teeth and
drummed his fingers irritably on the edge of the steering-
wheel. He was only ten minutes from home now and he
wanted to see the twins, before they went to school.
He'd only come this way round to drop the boy off and
it wasn't usually nose to tail. There must be a breakdown
or something, further on.

'I'll try and turn round,' he told Stan. 'There's a bit of
a dual carriageway coming up in a minute. I could just
about do it. I can go through Latchford, it'll be quicker
than waiting. OK?' But the boy seemed very jumpy all
of a sudden. He was sitting bolt upright in the cab now,
still holding on to his shabby old rucksack like grim
death; his fingers had turned white with the effort of
holding it so close to his chest. You'd have thought it
contained half a million in used notes. And his eyes kept
flicking sideways, down on to the heads of people in the
road as they walked to work. Something was wrong with
him.

'Like to come home with me, for a bit of breakfast?'
Jack said, as they edged forwards. He'd not been going
to offer that, it was a special time when he got home
from a long trip, a family time. And he wasn't at all sure

that he shouldn't have a word with someone about this boy, after his cock-and-bull story of someone chasing him. It almost certainly wasn't his father. He'd probably got himself into some kind of trouble with the police. Whatever it was, he'd been petrified when he'd done that crazy jump into the cab, and he was petrified still. He wasn't sixteen either, nothing like.

'Why don't you?' he repeated. 'Chris'll give you a good breakfast, it'll keep you going for a bit.'

'No thanks,' Stan said, as they jerked to a stop again. 'I can get out here. Don't bother about me. Did you say it was straight over the bridge?'

'Yes. That's Bridge Foot, and there's old Oliver Cromwell, pointing in the gutter at his lost half-crown. It's older than me, that statue is.'

'And I can get up there to the station?'

'Yes. You go into the centre of town, and straight across, and it's down Buttermarket Street, on the right. *Central* Station you want, not Bank Quay, that's for the inter-city trains . . . thought you said you'd been to Warrington?'

'It was a long time ago,' Stan muttered as he clambered down on to the pavement and slung the rucksack up on to his back again. Like when he was born.

'Got money for the train, have you?' Jack shouted, edging off slowly. A truck behind was hooting for him to get a move on but he was still reluctant to part with this boy.

'A bit,' Stan lied. Well, what else could he tell him? The fat lorry-driver had been kind but he felt that he was closing in on him now, with all these questions. He needed to go to earth for a bit, here, in this grotty-looking town, lose himself for a few hours and plan his next move. So he started walking.

If Julius was in that traffic jam too he'd have to stay there for a bit, and he easily could be. The truck had had 'Warrington and St Helens' painted on the side, large as

60

life. All Ratface had to do was to tail it. He must have got hold of a car because he'd complained of doing 'two hundred bloody miles up and down the motorway', looking for Stan. He must have added a few more since then, still hunting, unless he'd given up. The thought of Julius in this same town made Stan go cold for a minute, but he shrugged it off. It was fifty-fifty he'd gone to St Helens instead. Wherever that was.

He walked rapidly across the double bridge, the Mersey swirling its brown-grey waters under his boots, and passed Oliver Cromwell pointing down into the gutter. It was a very long shot, Julius being on to him already, but he still couldn't afford to take any risks. So long as he remained in this town he'd got to stay in the open, mix with people, in places where Julius couldn't go for him.

Stan was putting himself at risk too, because of that picture in the paper, but he reasoned that a boy missing from his foster home was a very little fish indeed compared with the great Julius Lodge; a boy like that was just a nuisance really.

It was the story of his life.

The town looked nothing much, and nearly all of it was new. He wandered round for hours, just staring into shop windows and leaning in doorways, watching the place fill up with shoppers. It could have been their own shopping precinct at home, with its Marks and Spencer's and its Boots and its Pizzaland, all glossy green paint and ferns. Auntie Marjorie had taken them to Pizzaland on his last birthday, for a treat. They did great meals there.

He'd eaten the remains of his food in Jack Brierley's lorry and he was hungry now. A boy came out of a snack bar with a hamburger and chips and he watched him stuff it down greedily, tomato sauce running out of his mouth. His own mouth was watering and the smell of the food was driving him crazy. He should have gone home for breakfast with that lorry-driver; he couldn't hold out forever. What must it be like in the really poor countries out in Africa, where people went for days without any food at all? Stan had never really thought about it till that moment.

A bus pulled up at a stop on the opposite pavement and someone in the queue yelled, 'Geoff! Get a move on, can't you?' The boy shoved the remains of the hamburger bun into his mouth and pelted across the road, scattering chips into the gutter. Stan stared at them for a long time, then he bent down and stretched out a hand nervously, looking along the street to see if anyone was watching. In his hunger he'd forgotten Julius.

There were eyes on him, but they weren't the cold blue eyes of Julius Lodge, they belonged to a little girl. She was standing outside a shoeshop while her mother looked in the window, tugging at her hand impatiently. The small mouth puckered distastefully as he scooped up a handful of chips, then she said loudly, 'That's dirty, that is. You're *dirty!*', and she pointed at him.

Her mother turned round and stared, then she drew the child towards her. Stan let the food drop through his fingers, straightened up and started brushing his jeans down, trying to shrug the moment off. But, just for a second, this woman's curious eyes had met his and he felt his cheeks burning. It shouldn't have been like this, his journey to Ireland, Julius Lodge on his back and the police, and someone nicking all his savings, him scrabbling in the gutter for someone else's abandoned food. He hated it.

'That boy was going to eat those chips,' the little girl chirped up.

'Er, could you tell me where the library is, please?' Stan said desperately. She'd got a very loud voice for such a little girl and people had started staring. He looked like what he was, someone far from home who'd been on the road all night. And they had printed that photo of him in the London paper. What if it had made the nationals too?

'The library?'

'Yes. We've got to look things up. You know, for school.'

'It's in Museum Street,' she told him suspiciously, gathering the child up. 'Come on, Emma. You go down there, then left, and it's right at the end, round the corner.' It was obvious that she didn't believe him. He ought to be in school surely, and he didn't come from round here, not with that accent. He was a bit rough-looking.

'Thanks.'

Stan started walking into the old part of the town, through a leafy square where accountants and solicitors had their offices. Cars were lined up nose to tail along the pavement but the black Mini was only cruising. Parking didn't matter yet.

Julius smiled to himself as he saw Stan push through the revolving doors of the library, and go inside. He was a fast operator. It hadn't taken him long to phone Gibbs Transport and the girl had given him the fat lorry-driver's home number straight away. It was in Warrington, not St Helens; piece of luck number one. He'd rung Jack Brierley and pretended to be Stan's dad; he'd taken a hard line with him, irresponsible, he'd said, giving a lift to a kid like that who just wanted a good hiding, and a lot more rubbish. The man had blustered, and ended up apologizing, but Julius hadn't listened to that. All he wanted to know was where the boy was making for next, and it was Liverpool. Piece of luck number two.

An hour or so's careful driving round this dump had paid off rather quicker than Julius had expected. He didn't need to go any further because here he was, large as life. What the hell was the boy doing in a library though? Typical of a creep like that, he'd always got his nose stuck in a book at Victor's.

There wouldn't be a back entrance for the public in a library and in any case the boy hadn't noticed him, so he could afford to relax for a minute.

He pulled up, dead opposite the revolving doors, and lit a cigarette.

Stan felt calmer inside. It was cool and quiet and nobody bothered him. At the main reception desk a solitary man sat writing on little white cards and in an upstairs room he could hear someone hoovering.

A large part of the hall was filled with an exhibition called 'Warrington as it Was', enlarged sepia photographs mainly, on metal stands, showing bits of the old town that had been pulled down to make the new shopping precinct. One section was labelled 'The Past Preserved'. It showed a network of little terraced streets with high-rise flats standing guard above them like concrete giants. 'These artisan dwellings of the mid nineteenth-century,' a notice explained, 'have been extensively renovated and modernized and are still lived in today often by the descendants of the men for whom they were built. Others, saved from demolition by the conservationists, are scheduled for the same caring restoration.'

Stan's eyes ran idly over the blurred photographs. He'd seen things like this before, in London, in museums they'd been to with school. Hundreds of houses got patched up down South. It was nothing to write home about, it was just a way of saving money. Then he saw it, a sign on the end of a terrace over a newsagent's shop that advertised Gold Cut. It said Chorley Street.

Chorley Street. It was where *she*'d come from, his mother, and the sister called Dawn whom Sid hadn't much liked. So it hadn't been flattened under a new road or one of those glaring white tower blocks, it was still there, shabby and small and 'lived in today, often by the descendants of . . .' Perhaps his own grandfather had lived in Chorley Street and been a tanner, or brewer of ale. They made beer in Warrington, vodka as well. The lorry-driver had told him that.

The muddy spider's web of little streets on the brown map looked quite near the old town centre, and there was a railway line to the right of it, marked 'Liverpool-Manchester'. So the black square in the middle must be Central Station, where the local trains went from.

Stan couldn't get to Liverpool on the train, even if he'd wanted to, because he had no money now. He'd only pretended to listen to Jack Brierley's instructions, just in case someone official came round, asking questions. What he ought to do was to start walking out of Warrington, till he hit the motorway again, then hitch another lift. It was only a mile or so away, according to these maps.

But his eyes kept going back to that little sign over the newsagent's shop, *Chorley Street*, black on pock-marked white. Mellor might have lived in Chorley Street too, Mellor, the man who'd fathered him. Someone might still live in Chorley Street who'd once known the invisible Mellor. Or her. Or him.

Half-dazed through the lack of sleep and food, but also because a strange, unexpected resolve was tightening up inside him, Stan moved back dopily to the revolving doors, one muddled foot treading on the other, making him totter slightly, like a drunk. He thought he'd stopped caring about all that long ago, where he'd come from and who he was, the one-night stand that had produced him so casually and, as casually, let him go.

But he hadn't destroyed those dimly imagined memories, or the great want that always came with them, the irrational longing to be united with an unknown woman with an unknown face, to have the same arms wrapped round him again that had opened once, only to let him be taken away. He had simply locked them up, sealed them in the uttermost dark of his mind, because what they meant was too painful for him.

Chorley Street. The black letters still danced across his eyes as he pushed through the doors into the sunlight. It was quite close. He was going to walk through the town and look at it.

He saw Julius straight away, leaning on the car roof with his skinny arms folded, pulling on a cigarette. But instead of going back through the revolving doors, or running off into a side-street, Stan walked straight towards him, and stopped in the middle of the road. Very casually, as if he had all the time in the world, Julius threw the cigarette into the gutter and ground it in with his heel. Then he opened the car door, flicked an inside lock and slammed it shut again, pocketing the keys.

A van came round the corner, screeched to a halt and hooted. Stan jumped out of the way but he still didn't get back on to the pavement. There were quite a few people here and as long as he stayed in a crowd he reckoned Ratface wouldn't dare go for him. Hooking his thumbs under the shoulder-straps of the rucksack he set off at a fast walk, back towards the new shopping area, keeping to the crown of the road, upright and almost defiant.

With a sick grin Julius started walking too, not hurrying yet but never letting the bulky, untidy figure in the dirty green anorak out of his sight. Catching up with the boy and getting what he wanted was only a matter of time now, but the place was important because Julius couldn't afford to draw attention to himself. He knew that Stan had figured that out for himself, and the knowledge didn't please him at all. When he'd finally cornered him he just might give him something to think about, before he let him go. The boy was asking for it.

Stan did the round of the shopping precinct yet again, endlessly, trying to shake Julius off, but he couldn't lose him. If he stared into a window he could see a small dark figure reflected in the glass and when he moved on it always moved with him. He went in and out of big stores and rode up and down on the escalators, shoppers tut-tutting at him bad-temperedly when the bulky rucksack blocked their way. But always, at his back, Julius came too, in a watchful, unnerving silence, never taking those cold blue eyes off him. At last he sat down for a minute on a bench, in a glossy paved area filled with plants where a fountain played, next to a chatty woman with four children who told him she was waiting for her husband to collect her, and the shopping. Julius appeared from a coffee bar, sat opposite and started to talk to one of the toddlers, amusing him with exaggerated noises. Yet he hated young people. At Auntie Marjorie's he'd said some filthy things to Stan and Elspeth, when she was out of earshot. Stan loathed him for what he was doing now. The soft baby face turned trustingly towards a man like Julius Lodge sickened him and he stood up abruptly, diving through some double glass doors into the open street again. It was the first time the boy had appeared to be hurrying and Julius, with a certain satisfaction, took it for panic and quickened his own pace.

Stan had decided to go to the station and try and get on a train. It didn't matter where it went. With no ticket he'd have to dodge the guard anyway, and get out as soon as it stopped. But he could go on to the platform and stick close to the other passengers till a train showed up, then he could follow someone on board and jump off again at the last minute if Julius followed him. It was a loony idea, the kind of stuff you saw in old films on the telly, but it might work. What else could he do?

He'd got a stitch now because he'd panicked and broken into a run. Ratface was running too. All the shoppers must be concentrated in the glossy new precinct because Buttermarket Street was like the grave. The man would go for him here if he didn't stick to the centre of the road.

'What are you bloody well playing at?' a voice yelled and a van appeared from nowhere, slewing to a stop, and denting its rear end into a parked car. 'Trying to get yourself killed or something?' Stan didn't stop running but when he flicked his head round he could see the van-driver getting out of his seat, grabbing Julius by the shoulder. 'It was the boy . . .' he heard. 'It's nothing to do with me, mate, I was just minding my own business, that's what I was doing . . .' But the driver kept him arguing, long enough for Stan to gain more ground. He tore past Central Station and plunged up a narrow side-street into the old terraced part of the town where the rebuilding was going on. It'd be trickier to find him in a place like this, he decided, than on a half-empty station platform. That had been a mad idea. It had been a sort of miracle, the van-driver grabbing Julius like that and keeping him talking, and it had saved him. For the first time in what felt like years Stan decided that he really was on his own again.

For a good hour he walked the little streets, only stopping to look behind and to listen for signs of Julius. There were far more old houses here than he'd thought, from those maps in the library, and the place was a lot messier. Exhibitions always made things look clean and tidy when they weren't in real life. Stan thought the place was more like a bomb-site than anything else. There were small mountains of debris not cleared away near the glaring white high-rise flats, and old houses left half-demolished. Chorley Street ought to be round here somewhere but he couldn't find it. Perhaps it had turned out too rotten to be worth preserving and ended up as a heap of broken bricks. Those conservation photos in the library were probably out of date by now.

It was quiet in the little streets and Julius had obviously lost him. The sick tight feeling in his stomach eased a little and he wandered about rather aimlessly, looking for a place to sit down. Nerves and hunger were playing havoc with him now and his legs felt wobbly, as if they didn't quite belong to him.

The low smartened-up terraces seemed to go on forever and they all looked the same with their uniform grey-green doors and their new plastic drainpipes. From Egypt Street he turned into Cairo Place, then on to Inkerman Street, then Pharaoh Street. And suddenly the streets became flowers and he was on Crocus Walk, Tulip Walk and Narcissus Way. The houses here looked newer and bigger, and they'd got tiny gardens.

At last the terraces ended and he was in another weedy space, half-cleared for rebuilding. They were still tearing down the old back-to-backs here. He could see a naked gable-end with its little black grate perched halfway up the wall and a blodged brown line where the floor had been.

There were a few old oil-drums in the middle of the patch and a heap of broken bricks. Stan's legs felt as if they were turning to water underneath him and he went over to the oil-drums and flopped down in a heap.

Somewhere in the city a bell struck twelve. Two men cycled down the streets that flanked his patch and a little kid in dungarees came out of a backyard and started grubbing in the dirt.

Now he'd stopped, and allowed his body to relax a bit, his hunger came creeping back and, worse than hunger, thirst. His lips and throat were papery for lack of something to drink. All he'd had was the lukewarm coffee, sickly sweet, and that was hours ago. He longed for a cup of cold water.

Suddenly he delved into a side pouch on the rucksack, and got his red notebook out. 'Sept. 20th,' he wrote, 'I'm in Warrington, surprise surprise. A lorry-driver gave me a lift and he lives here. Julius came after me in a service station. Nearly killed myself getting away. That packet Victor's after –' Then he stopped writing. He had seen the shiny black panel of a car door slide past an opening where two terraces met. Then it came again, passing and repassing, and somebody a few houses away was unwinding a window rapidly, to get a better view.

Julius. Stan's eyes zeroed in on the face, seeing it large and magnified, like the Bionic Man. The whiskers, the sandy bristles, the large nose. The slack mouth half-open showing little pointed teeth. Ratface.

He straightened up and stared down the alley to where the Mini door was a shiny black square. The kid in dungarees was kicking at a punctured football now. Julius shouldered past him slowly.

Stan had unlaced the heavy boots when he'd first sat down, and eased his painful feet out of them. Now he stood in his socks on the mud of the waste ground. He stopped only to fasten the rucksack and swing it up on to his shoulders again. Julius had already reached the end of the alley.

The boy turned and ran. The bare patch in the middle of the terraces was a litter of broken glass and rubble. Before he was clear of it one sock was cut to ribbons and he left little splodges of red where he pelted across the road that edged the waste land, diving into a thin blackness between two high walls. Out of the sun the dark shadow gaped at him like a huge chopped-off vein.

The alleyway was long, twenty, perhaps thirty houses, and the snatch of light at the other end was a long time growing into anything. But at last he gained the end wall and stopped, gobbling for breath, jerking his head back along the black line of smoke-furred granite slabs that shored off the tiny backyards like so many tombstones. Julius was half-way down the row already and gaining on him.

Stan burst out again into a bright street, Egypt, Cairo, Narcissus. It could be any. He ran straight across and a bicycle wheel grazed him. The machine wobbled and somebody fell off.

'Fer cryin' out loud . . . what the *hell*!' It was a little old man in a flat cap. Julius danced round him like a boxer, trying to push past, but Stan had gone.

Down an entry with washing lines strung from wall to wall like bunting. Through the shredded socks Stan felt the small bumps of cobbles. Shirts and pillowcases slapped wetly at his face and he struggled to get through. *Go back*. But turning he saw Julius fill the mouth of the entry. It was dank, shadowy and the sun had gone in. There was nobody about.

The thin man slid something out from under his jacket and Stan heard a click; he was moving up fast now. The boy tugged at a rope looped over a crumbling iron hook and the washing line gave way. He gained half a minute while Julius disentangled himself from the dripping folds of a shabby striped bedspread.

Out of the entry. He looked left and saw a vast acreage of rubble and earth. Brick mountains greened over with weeds. No cover. Right. An abandoned street half torn down. Great timber buttresses propped up the front walls and there were gaps where doors had hung.

He passed through a doorway and snatched the place in with greedy eyes. Small eddies of brick rubble under his bleeding feet, smashed doors and window-frames, huge concrete lumps that had been beams. In the middle a complication of low walls, somehow not flattened.

He clambered over to them and crouched in the shadows. Inside the roofless house someone had cleared a space big enough to lie down, and he could smell earth and urine. A piece of corrugated iron had been dragged on top of the walls for shelter but now flapped about crazily.

Through a hole in the iron sheet Stan could see Julius. It was very quiet. The traffic on a nearby road thinned down to a hum, children's voices were only squeaks. Stan could hear the sheeting creak as a tiny wind moved it.

The man was looking down at something in his

outstretched palm, jerking his head back now and then, to check the street, then leaning against the door-jamb again. Just waiting.

Stan's heart was half-way to his throat, and pounding painfully. His ears were sore and it felt as if blood was pouring out of them. He concentrated on Julius's head through the rusty hole, screwing his eyes up hard so that the water filled them. Now he'd stopped running the pain in his feet was agony, and he glanced down at the bloodsoaked socks.

A large grey rat had crept out from under some bricks and was inches away from him; its body quivered and Stan saw fleas rippling through its fur.

It crept up to his feet, sniffling at the bloody rags of his socks, its tail brushed his anorak in a string of slime. Little teeth flashed and the rat began to pull at the socks, tearing and tearing.

Stan let out a scream and stood up. The corrugated sheet fell over and clashed down on to the bricks. In the doorway Julius jerked into sudden life like a marionette.

The boy pushed through the rubble towards a bit of rear wall where a door, still with its paint on, hung foolishly. As the blistered panels swung back Stan heard a loud cracking noise; the place rang with it and a brick clattered down from a half-demolished chimney. Now there was a sharp burning smell.

He was back in the tombstone alley and the sky a ribbon of cloudy blue netted with aerials and wires, but it was empty and he ran down. Julius fired again and the black walls rang back at him, magnifying the sound. At the end he turned left. More backs, the way through narrower. Half-way down there was a dustbin daubed with white paint.

Stan leapt on to it, vaulted over a decrepit gate into a small backyard and crouched down. Seconds later light footsteps went pattering past.

He waited there for a full five minutes, then he pulled

himself up the gate and peered along the alley. Two women stood talking at the end and one was pointing down the street, away from him. Then, as though in a nightmare now, not knowing whether the noise was real or not, Stan heard the light footsteps coming back.

At the end of the yard he saw a back door. He crept over to it and started hammering.

'That you, Vera?'

'Yes, yes it's me,' Stan said dumbly, in a dry whisper.

There was a sound of furniture being scraped back, then a slow key turning, but he couldn't wait. When a slit showed he pushed with his shoulder and got himself inside. Whipping around he slid home the bolts, then turned the key again.

Stan slid down the door in a heap, his feet turning the rag-rug into a concertina. The old woman cowered away from him. In a corner by the gas cooker she hid her face in her hands and started to scream.

Chapter Eight

The cracked cries sounded horribly loud, like huge bells clashing in a tiny room. Stan got up from the floor and went over to her.

'Don't,' he said. '*Don't*. It's OK.'

She was small, flattish, her body had folded in two like paper. Her hands covered her face completely, blue-ribboned and thin. Gradually the shrieks turned into a low keening.

He prised at the fingers, trying to unstick them from her face.

'Someone's after me,' he said, 'and I had to shake him off. I'm not after anything, honest to God.'

He stood away from her, opening his hands, and she got up slowly, hanging on to the cooker. Then she gave him a long silent stare. Small eyes, warm brown, in a crumpled face, thick white hair, newly washed and set.

'What's in that bag then?'

'Nothing much. Only my stuff.'

'Show me.'

'OK.'

He undid all the straps and tipped the contents of his rucksack on to the red kitchen tiles, everything except the plastic packet; he'd zipped that into an inside pouch.

The old woman never took her eyes off him but she was turning the pile over slowly, with one foot.

'What's that then? Your diary?'

'Sort of. I write things down in it.'

She was still staring. Stan stared back and pulled the woolly hat off. His matted curls, full of blood cakes, sprang out. There was a big sticking plaster over his left eye, his face was filthy and he'd got blood all over his hands.

But his feet had stopped hurting. The soles of his socks had disintegrated completely now and he stood barefoot; the kitchen tiles were cool to the sores and cuts.

'You look a sight, don't you?'

He said nothing.

'Well, you do, don't you, coming in here making your mess.' She sounded like a schoolteacher, ticking him off. Stan hung his head, like a child.

Very cautiously she made her way past him. The house had two ground-floor rooms, with the kitchen part stuck on at the back, and he followed her into a little sitting-room.

'Fire needs seeing to now,' she clucked, hen-like, and got down on her knees with difficulty, ignoring Stan, as if she'd forgotten all about him.

He said, 'Here, I'll do it.'

He was good at making fires and he squatted down next to her and got to work with the poker, putting on a few knobs of coal then rearranging it all. He shovelled slack on the back and poked again. At last the fire blazed and spat. As he straightened up the room seemed to darken slightly. He was dizzy now and he clutched at the fireplace to steady himself.

'You'd better sit down, hadn't you?' she said, noticing, and she nudged him towards a chair, seating herself opposite in an old rocker.

It was raining now and the little room looked dark, though she'd got the electric light on. Stan glanced up at it, a china bowl on three chains, furred with the grease of years and choked with cobwebs and dead moths.

'I thought it was our Vera. She'll be here in a minute.

She'll know what to do.' She was talking more to herself than to Stan.

Silence. He sweated inside the anorak and unzipped it suddenly. The noise went through the old woman and she jumped. It seemed so dark and the sky outside looked pale brown; he could hardly see.

'I could get that light down for you. We could clean it.'

'Can't get up there. I've got bad legs,' she confided.

Stan understood bad legs, Mrs Kelly had had them too. She was a large woman, mountainous as she got older, and she'd wheeze round the tiny flat doing all the cleaning, grunting with pain. Stan and Sid had done everything for her towards the end.

'Let me give it a clean,' he said. 'I know how.'

She watched as he spread an old newspaper on the table, climbed up and stood there, carefully unhooking the bowl from its chains and taking the bulb out; everything was softly furred with thick dust.

'Look, I can wash this, and wipe the bulb for you, then you'll get a proper light, see?'

He showed her the glass bowl and drew a line in the dust but she shrank away from him, suspicious of the mop of tousled hair, the bloody feet. Her small face was hard, still blank and only half-trusting. Stan went into the tiny back kitchen and ran water into the sink. The scullery was minute but as neat as a pin. He dried the bowl with a clean tea-towel, neatly folded, and wiped the bulb with a bit of the newspaper.

The light fitting was soon replaced and switched on again. Brightness poured into the room and the old woman blinked and looked round her. For the first time she gave him a tiny little smile.

'That's champion, that is, you're a good lad you are.' Then she added again, 'Our Vera'll be here soon. She'll know what to do.'

But she no longer seemed so frightened of him. It was

as if she had forgotten the terror of his sudden appearance and was remembering only one thread, that he was in trouble.

'That's my book on the dresser,' she said confidingly as Stan started to put everything back in his rucksack; she was watching him slide the red notebook down into the back pocket of his jeans. 'You can have a look at it, if you want.'

Stan took the fat scrapbook off the dresser and sat down at the table. It was a book of newspaper cuttings going back twenty or thirty years. There were dozens of photographs of the Royal Family at weddings and race meetings and launching ships, all carefully labelled and dated in a careful copperplate handwriting. There were snaps from the local paper of school speechdays and gold watch presentations, and processions on something called 'Walking Day'. At the back he found a series of newspaper articles cut from the big dailies. He puzzled over them for quite a while then suddenly realized that they were all about one thing.

She'd framed one column thickly in bright blue biro. The headline said: *Widow near death after beating* and he read:

> *An eighty-one-year-old widow was fighting for her life in hospital last night after being attacked in the front garden of her home in Warrington; Mrs Edna May Hughes has severe head and face injuries after what police describe as a 'wicked and vicious systematic beating'. They believe –*

'She died, Edna May.' The old woman's voice cut into him. 'My best friend she was. I was Mary Ellen and she was Edna May. We started school together in Standard One. When you pushed the door open I thought – '

Stan understood. Closing the book carefully he put it back on the dresser. Then he opened his mouth to say that he was very sorry, but the words felt silly and weak. He swallowed them back.

'We don't need the light on, do we? It's fining up now.' Stan got out of the chair to find the switch and at the same moment the yard gate rattled and a thin shadow barred the window. *Julius*. They'd not rebuilt the small pathetic barrier of kitchen furniture that the old woman had heaped against the door, in case someone should break in and beat her about the head, like Edna May.

Fear flushed along Stan's veins and his mouth went completely dry.

'Sit you down, it's only our Vera,' and she went through the scullery to open the door.

Vera looked a lot younger than her sister Mary, and she was oddly dressed. Underneath her long navy gaberdine she was clothed completely in black and she wore a black straw bonnet tied with broad black ribbon. Across the front on a red band it said 'Salvation Army' in white letters. The two women sat on opposite sides of the fire with Stan between them, perched on a hard chair, and the atmosphere, which had become easier as he'd stoked the fire and looked at the scrapbook, felt colder again, more hostile. Sister Vera had a stare so hard and unforgiving it made his heart sink. She was obviously getting ready to ask a whole load of awkward questions.

But Mary got in first. 'How old do you think I am?' she wanted to know; her voice was stronger and more confident now her sister was there to protect her, and she seemed to be rather enjoying the extra company. Stan hesitated. She looked about a hundred.

'I don't know,' he said. 'Seventy perhaps? Really, I don't know.'

'Get off with you! Eighty-three I'll be, next July. Our Vera's the baby of the family. How old d'you think she is?'

'Oh, leave off, Mary,' the other woman snapped impatiently. 'I'm seventy-six. No secret about that. The boy's not interested anyway. Are you?' She was looking at him keenly.

'I wasn't there when the brains were given out,' Mary prattled on, 'no good at figures me. But *that one* – teacher, she was, grammar school girl,' she added proudly. 'No time for the fellers, ran too fast for them to keep up with her, that's what our Jack used to say. There's our Jack,' and she pointed to a blurred brown wedding photograph on the mantelpiece.

'We only had the one child, George. He's in Canada, doing well. I've got three grandchildren and one great grandson, Georgie they called him, after his grandad. That's them.' Another photo, this time a large family group in a leather frame.

'Look, Vera, doesn't he favour our Georgie, this one?' She pointed to a tall well-made boy with thick curly hair, holding a puppy.

The severe-looking woman in the black straw bonnet nodded vaguely, still looking hard at Stan, but her sister said happily, 'I like this boy, he's got a nice way with him,' as if he wasn't in the room.

'Mary tells me you ran in here because someone was after you?' The tall angular woman shot the sharp question at him like firing a pistol. 'Don't you think you'd better explain yourself?'

Stan crumpled inside. There'd be no getting past this kind of woman with a vague story. A vision of all the teachers, matrons and social workers he had ever known rolled up before him in a cloud of disapproval, and strict truth. Lies wouldn't work with her.

It was looking hopeless and he began to think he'd never get to Ireland now, never see Sid and Mrs Kelly's brother. Everything was closing in on him again though he reckoned he could have got round Mary, if Vera hadn't turned up. She was old and her mind wandered. She'd already forgotten how he'd burst in on her and she was obviously mixing him up with Georgie now, the curly-haired boy in Canada.

But Vera was tougher. That gaunt, unsmiling figure had obviously been in the world more. 'Salvation Army' meant that she was very religious indeed. There was a boy at school called Roland Hayter whose mother wore a straw bonnet just like this, and he wasn't allowed to do anything the others did; they didn't even have TV. Why did being Christian mean you had to be so miserable? Vera reminded him a bit of Auntie Marjorie.

She didn't really sound very northern when she spoke, whereas Mary's accent was thick, like someone out of 'Coronation Street'. It sounded as if she'd lived all her life in the same house.

Vera was waiting, drumming her fingers on the arm of her chair, so Stan started, selecting his facts very carefully.

First he told her about Auntie Marjorie fostering him, and the places he'd been in before that, and how he'd decided to try and find Sid in Ireland. Then he told her about Victor showing up with Julius Lodge, and making it clear he wasn't welcome, and how he'd decided to leave home. He didn't mention the two fights with Kingsley. There was no way he could explain to a woman like this how he'd felt about Mrs Kelly, or how Kingsley's mockery had made him faint with rage.

'This old lady who looked after you for a while,' the grim woman in black said severely. 'That sounds very odd to me. It's not at all the usual practice. How old were you?'

'Seven. She was only going to have us for a few weeks while they were finding us somewhere else. She'd looked after loads of children. Then there was a new social worker took over and she didn't catch up with the arrangement, I suppose. We stayed there anyhow.'

'For how long?'

'Three years, just over. The woman who'd sent us

there was moved to another district and the new person didn't come round very often. We were OK anyhow. It was great at her place.'

'And why did you leave her?'

'She was ill and anyway – '

Stan stopped suddenly. The inside of his throat felt like a raw wound and a lump was blocking it. His eyes swam, turning the garish carpet pattern to a soft blur.

He knew he should never have gone back to Mrs Kelly's street. After he'd had the fights with Kingsley he'd skipped school and gone back to his old haunts, looking for her house. He'd had to *know*. In four years with Auntie Marjorie he'd never allowed himself to go anywhere near the place she'd lived in because he did know, really.

Their street had looked a bit like it did round here, with most of the houses pulled down for rebuilding but with odd patches left, here and there. Mrs Kelly's flat was on the top floor of a house that had been somehow forgotten by the demolition squad. Next door was still stuck on it but together they stood up like a slab of cake with everything around them flattened. Stan thought it must have always been like that; he couldn't ever remember a whole street, or looking out on to other houses, only a waste of rubble stretching away.

Nor could he remember how he first got there, or whether Sid had always been with him, or if he came a bit later. But at Mrs Kelly's they had been together, *brothers*. They went off to school together and when they came home to the flat she was always there, waiting for them.

Once or twice a woman came from the Child Welfare department, asking a lot of questions. It worried Stan. But Sid explained that they'd only come to see if the two boys were being looked after properly, if the house was clean and stuff, and whether they got enough to eat. Well, the flat was so bright and shiny you could have eaten your dinners off the floor. And she was a fantastic cook. Stan could still smell the richness of meat and spuds simmered for hours in a glistening brown pot, the tarts and drop scones, the brown moist soda bread that she said you always got to eat in Ireland.

Bright rags of memory broke away and floated across the grey of his vision. He saw Mrs Kelly moving slower and slower round the flat on her bad legs, singing to herself as she polished and tidied up, having a crack with her cronies from the old days who'd been moved out to the new flats, brown stout bottles lined up on the table like rows of polished organ pipes. He saw the day she ordered a Radio Taxi and turned up at school for a concert, sitting proudly in the front row looking out for Sid and Stan. He saw her best green coat and her best green hat. Everyone had giggled and someone said, 'Is that your gran then, Stan?' and he'd said 'Yes.' He knew she wouldn't mind.

He remembered the warmth, the clean sheets on his own bed, the food she made them, the home smell. Nobody else was there, fighting to get her attention. Mrs Kelly was theirs, someone of their own.

Voices were worst. Hers was coming back to him in the room. Now loud, a cackling hoot of laughter. Now soft, like Irish rain. At first he'd been little enough to creep into her lap and snuggle up, and Sid would sit close too.

'She is a procession no one can follow after,
But be like a little dog following a brass band.'

He should not have gone back.

They'd still not started building the new street but when he looked along it from the old familiar corner, the slice-of-cake house had gone. All he could find was a mound of rubble a fresher pink than the piles around it which were brown and crusted over. He knew it was their house because the pattern of cracks in the pavement by Mrs Kelly's front door was in the shape of a boat with a little sail. He always looked out for it.

The breath had gone out of him like when Victor had put the boot in under the table. He'd stayed out for hours that day, waiting till the pain inside had dulled down to a slow ache. But if his mind crept over to it everything flared out again, like the quick pain when you rip a plaster off raw, unhealed flesh, and it would not go away.

'What happened?'

The firm voice pushed him on, a shade kinder than he'd thought at first. Or was he imagining it?

'She started to lose weight and they took her into hospital. She had a growth or something.'

'Cancer?'

'I suppose so.' *Why did she have to say it?*

'And what happened to you and your brother?'

'We went to a Centre for a bit – that's where you go sometimes, while they're finding someone to take you permanently.'

'I know that,' she said crisply. 'And then what happened?'

'I was sent to Auntie Marjorie's. Sid didn't come, he'd already left school. She – Mrs Kelly – she kept her promise. Her brother Joe came over from Ireland and Sid went back with him to work on their farm. They all came to see me once. They brought us some potatoes.'

'Do they know you're on your way to them, the people on this farm? Does your brother know?'

Stan shook his head then said quickly, before she asked anything else, 'It'll be all right though.'

But Vera's lips were pursed tightly together in a thin line. She looked doubtful.

'You seem very sure. *Why?* Has your brother mentioned it at all? Are they expecting you?'

He hesitated. 'Well . . . not exactly. I mean, we didn't agree a date or anything.'

'So you do write to him then, this brother in Ireland?'

'Yes. Of course I do.'

'And he writes back.'

'*Yes.*'

Sort of. Scrappy little notes now and again, in reply to all those pages that Stan wrote. He was the solid, boring one, and Sid was the whiz-kid with the motor bikes and the girlfriends. 'Farming life won't suit you for ever, Sid.' Joe had said that himself the time they came over with the potatoes. Perhaps, when he did get there, Stan would find he wasn't so welcome after all. Sid might even have moved out and found a job in town. It was months since his last letter.

He'd never really allowed himself to think about the practical details of turning up at the farm, out of the blue, it was simply a dream he'd had. Dreams were better than life at Auntie Marjorie's. Vera was forcing him to look at the whole plan much closer now, and he didn't want to, because of what it might mean. The thin unyielding figure in the funny straw bonnet had sown the first seeds of real doubt.

'Have you got the immersion on, Mary?' she said snappily.

The older sister had been staring at Stan with small, wet eyes. She jumped slightly, then nodded.

'This boy should have a hot bath. All these clothes need washing, or throwing away.' She looked distastefully at his socks.

'You can have a bath, chuck,' Mary said. 'I've got a bonny little bathroom now, the council put it in for me. And I'll find you something clean to put on.' She went through to the stairs, and Stan heard pipes clicking as a bath was being filled.

He glanced through the window. No movement in the yard except a sparrow perched on the back gate.

'Now, let's get this straight, shall we,' Vera started, as soon as Mary was out of earshot. 'Was there someone after you or not? She said there was but her memory's going. She lives in a dreamworld half the time.'

Stan stared at the floor in silence. Let her think what she wanted. She was against him and she'd probably report every word he said to the police. He'd be sent back to London, to a place worse than Auntie Marjorie's, and the whole business of being shunted here and there like a piece of unwanted baggage would start all over again. She mustn't do it, anything was better than being taken back into care. He'd got to reach Ireland, even if Sid had taken off. Mrs Kelly's brother would help him.

In sudden panic he grabbed at her cool thin fingers. 'Please don't go to the police,' he pleaded. 'I've not done anything wrong and I'll go tomorrow. You've got to believe me. I've told you the *truth*.' Religious people like her ought to stick up for boys like him, boys that were down on their luck and trying to make a break for themselves, striking out in a new direction. Salvation Army people believed in 'the blood of Christ', Roland Hayter had told him that, he'd given a talk about it in class. What did it mean if it didn't mean love? 'It's the truth,' he repeated in a whisper, withdrawing his hand.

The truth, the whole truth, and nothing but the truth. He hadn't told the whole truth, but then, she hadn't asked those questions.

There was a long silence then she said unexpectedly, 'I believe what you've told me, Stan. I don't doubt it's the truth. The Lord tells me it is.'

But he was sceptical. She just prides herself on being a good judge of character, he was thinking. Auntie Marjorie did too, but she was wrong sometimes. Look at Victor.

'I shan't be doing anything about you just at the moment anyway,' she went on. 'I'm on my way to an important church meeting and it's likely to last several hours. I only stopped to look at Mary. I know she'll be all right with you for a while, and you'll be all right here. She'll cook you a good meal and when I come back we'll talk. I'm not promising anything though. Something's got to be done with you.'

Chapter Nine

Mary soon had him sitting at the table. She seemed convinced now that Stan was her great grandson Georgie, who'd come over from Canada to see his Great Gran.

She said, 'I hope you don't mind having your meal early, chuck, but I usually do. Time goes that slow when you're on your own, and our Vera's not in to her tea today. Them prayer meetings go on for hours.'

Stan didn't mind at all. He'd had a long soak in a hot bath, washed his hair, lathered himself with Lifebuoy, then dried himself with luxurious slowness on a massive striped towel.

More than once he'd rubbed a spyhole in the steamed-up window-pane and peeped down into the tiny yard. The birds had gone but there was still no Julius. He was starting to breathe more easily again. Ratface must have lost him well and truly or he'd have shown up by now. That gave Stan a few hours to think, days even. He wasn't sure yet what he was going to do, it would all depend on what Vera said. She was formidable. He might have to slip away before she showed up again. She said she believed him but it didn't mean she wouldn't go to the police.

The clothes they'd found for him were very old-fashioned; grey flannels, checked shirt and a knitted Fair Isle pullover. The trousers were much too short but they looked all right with his socks pulled up over them. His boots would help too. Then he remembered. He hadn't got any boots, he'd left them by the oil-drums when he'd run away from Julius. So he padded downstairs in long woollen socks.

'Them were our Jack's things,' Mary said simply, bringing a pot through from the scullery. 'I couldn't bring myself to throw anything away. That must be why I was keeping them – for you. There's always a reason. That's what our Vera says, any road.'

They ate hot-pot with pickled red cabbage and a crust served in wedges on a separate plate, then there was thick rice pudding. She kept on filling his plate up.

'You must be clemmed, Georgie, what have they been feeding you on, down London?'

'Not much,' Stan mumbled, his mouth crammed.

'Bet it's not as good as your mam makes you, is it? Or that old lady who looked after you. What's her name?'

And she rambled on and on. It was obvious that she'd listened carefully to what Stan had told Vera, but now the details were hopelessly muddled. One minute she thought he was Georgie, the next a poor lad from down London way who needed looking after. It didn't really matter what Stan told her.

'My mother came from round here,' he said casually, when they were washing up in the scullery and she was boiling the kettle for a cup of tea.

'What was her name? I might know her. I had my own hairdresser's once. All the girls came to me when they had something special on.'

'It was years ago,' Stan said. 'You wouldn't have known her.'

'How do you know? What was her name, before she was married like?'

'Gleghorn, I think.'

'Gleghorn?' Mary was scornful. 'That's right common round here. There's some on Arthur Royd Street, and some on Crompton Avenue, and some on Cairo Street, no Chorley Street. Cousins they were, all related . . . but

I think they moved away.' She waggled her chin as she measured the tea out. 'Eee, them Gleghorns. A right pair of trollops they turned out to be, Dawn and Mavis. I can see 'em now. There were so many of 'em council let them have two houses and knocked 'em together. Now Mavis . . .' and she leaned over to him, dropping her voice to a whisper, 'she was a bit – y'know – mental-like. People say awful things, don't they? Any road, she kept on having babbies and her mam looked after them. She needed looking after herself, that girl did. Now when the mother passed away an auntie . . .'

But Stan had stopped listening. An uncanny, high-pitched whining was sounding in his head, blotting her voice out. He felt dizzy and sick. *Chorley Street.*

'I've seen our mum,' Sid had told him once, and Stan thought he remembered talk of another baby who could have been Elspeth, and a woman called Auntie Dawn whom Sid hadn't liked.

'I think she's a bit cracked,' was Sid's conclusion, and Mrs Kelly hadn't asked him any more questions. Stan, just nine, had only been interested for a few minutes. His mother hadn't sent them a present and she never came to see them. Warrington might as well be Australia, for all he cared.

'Will you cut my hair, Mary?' he said suddenly. He'd got an idea. The teacups were washed and on the drainer and they were sitting by the fire in the old chairs.

It was too hot for it really, the rain had petered out again and it was sunny in the backyard, but he was pulling at his collar.

'I'm so hot with all this hair, Mary. I should have had it seen to in London, but there wasn't time. You've not forgotten how to cut hair, have you?'

The idea obviously tickled her. She was already on her feet and scrabbling in a drawer.

'Don't you ever go near them barbers, Georgie, that's

89

my advice, not when your gran can do it. They're a right lot of twisters, they are.' She was already combing his hair out carefully.

'You shouldn't really have washed it, chuck,' she told him. 'You should have waited till after. I'll do my best, any road. Ee, me fingers are that stiff. Now keep *still*, love.'

She snipped and combed and clipped at him, tittering like a naughty little girl. 'What'd our Vera say, me doing this?' Stan wasn't the only one who was frightened of her. After ten minutes she made him get up and look in the big oval mirror over the sideboard.

'Will that do, chuck? I've not dared take much off.'

He stared at himself. It still looked too like him in the photo, there were far too many curls.

'Mary . . . *Gran* . . . can you keep a secret?'

She nodded, beaming at him.

'Someone's after me. Remember? That's why I ran here. Well, supposing my picture's in the papers and that man sees it? He's a real bad lot, Mary, and I've not done anything wrong, honest to God. I want you to cut off as much as you can, really flatten it. Otherwise they'll recognize me. C'mon, you're a hairdresser. Have a go.'

He sat down again. What would she make of the mad story? She seemed a bit mad herself, with the weak-mindedness of old age. Everything was becoming so unreal now; perhaps he was going mad too. Her hand was on his shoulder and he squeezed it lightly. 'It's my only chance, Mary, go on.'

She grieved gently as the thick curls showered down in gold bubbles on the carpet. Now she was into it properly she was not snipping but chopping, all over his head. It took a long time. After she'd finished with the scissors she ran clippers all over it, then over his neck, and round his ears. He felt shivery and cold suddenly, a lamb sheared of its winter fleece.

'Now I'm going to put some of this on.' She fetched a

bottle from a cupboard and poured something on his head, rubbing it in like shampoo.

'What's that?' It smelt sickly.

'Mind your own business. It'll flatten it good and proper, temporary like. Don't *wash* it though,' and she combed his hair carefully.

'I've finished, chuck. Ten and six that'll be.' She poked at him and cackled. 'Have a look at it.'

He looked like Siegfried out of that old vet series on the telly, only fatter. His hair was now a smooth yellow thatch with a neat side parting and an old-fashioned 'bang' on his forehead.

'It's great, it's really great. Thanks, Mary. Now, have you got any old glasses? That'd really do it.'

She click-clicked her tongue, pretending to disapprove. But she was pleased, captivated. Life hadn't been so interesting for a very long time. 'Glasses . . . glasses . . . bottom drawer. Have a look yourself, Georgie, there should be some.'

It was a man's drawer, very neat, full of old tins with labels on; 2-inch nails, staples, a magnifying glass, small tools. The first pair of spectacles was impossible. When he put them on the world turned to a pebbly blur. The second pair were much better. When he'd adjusted to the way things loomed up at him then shot away again it was all right. He must keep trying them on until they felt a part of him, like false teeth.

In the mirror he looked perfect. Pretty horrible. He just hoped he'd never have to wear glasses in real life.

Next to the fireplace there was a small cupboard with the door half-open. Stan spotted a pair of shoes pushed down at the back, under some newspapers, and he pulled them out. Boots, diamond-black with real leather laces, beautiful boots.

'I've got no shoes, Mary. I lost them when that man chased me. Could I have these, d'you think?'

The old lady looked at the boots for a long time. At

last she said flatly, 'If they fit you, chuck, have 'em. They were Jack's. I kept them, after.'

Like the rest of her husband's things they were a bit small for Stan but he squeezed his feet into them and began to lace them up. Mary kept looking at the clock.

'I generally put my feet up in the afternoons. But if you're going out fetch us some toffees.' She laughed. 'Our Vera says I eat too many sweets but I say to her, I don't smoke, I don't drink, I never go out.'

'I've no money,' Stan said.

'I'll give you some money, then I want to get my head down.' She seemed to be getting a bit restless with him, eager to have him out of the way for a while. Stan understood. Mrs Kelly hadn't liked anyone upsetting her routine either. It happened when you got old.

He followed her into the chilly front 'parlour' with its silent grandfather clock and all the chairs covered in dust-sheets. On a sideboard there was an old copper kettle. Mary took the lid off, rooted inside and brought out a roll of banknotes.

'I always keep a bit of money in here,' she told him. 'Our Vera thinks it's all in the post office but she doesn't know about this.' She tipped the kettle upside down and gave it a shake. 'I thought I'd got some fifty pences in here, but I've spent them evidently. Must have. Take one of these.' She peeled off a note and gave it to him.

'This is a tenner, Mary. Haven't you got any pound coins? It's only for sweets.'

'Oh, take it. They'll change it. Go to Green's, corner of Chorley Street. They'll still be open, they know me. And don't go waking me with your noise when you come back.'

She pinched at his cheek and smiled. 'Eh, you're bonny you are. You're a little belter.'

All the time Julius was on his tail Chorley Street had evaded him. Now he found it quite easily, not five minutes' walk from the house, and Green's was the little corner shop in the library photo, the one selling Gold Cut.

He went in and bought some humbugs. Old ladies seem to like mints, Mrs Kelly had always kept them in, for indigestion. He pushed all the change into the pocket of the baggy flannels, on top of the rolled-up notebook, shoving everything down with the knot of his knuckles. He knew for certain he would need the money soon. And yet. He'd left the old woman snoring trustfully on the settee, her teeth out. He would have to go back. He was Georgie.

Nailed on a battered fence outside the shop he saw a travel poster about the Liverpool to Dublin ferries. Two children were smiling out at him under the eye of a tanned Dad jiggling a tray of drinks. There seemed to be plenty of boats to Dublin. Some went to Northern Ireland too, to Belfast.

Stan was glad he'd be well away from a place like that, in the lush green peace of County Cork. There were always killings in Belfast, bombs going off, young soldiers turning mad in barracks with the strain and terror of it all. He'd seen those news stories on TV. The small print at the bottom of the poster listed sailing times, and connecting trains from Central Station. Stan felt for a pencil in the pocket of his trousers, then he remembered; they were Jack's. There was only the red notebook and Mary's money, so he'd have to try and memorize what it said.

He straightened up slowly, looking along the terraced street to someone only yards away. He'd not forgotten Julius Lodge, not for a minute, but he wasn't his own man any more. Something much stronger than the fear of Julius had driven him out, dream-like, to look for that house on Chorley Street.

There were eyes on him, huge, liquid brown in a dirty face. A little girl, three, perhaps four, had momentarily forgotten her pram full of dolls and was eyeing him curiously from the middle of the street. Stan's flattened thatch felt like a wig, his hands itched to pull it off, and the thick glass of the spectacles was making him feel slightly sick. Somehow he felt the child knew all about him, could see who he really was, and he started to sweat.

He walked down Chorley Street keeping to the very edge of the pavement, avoiding the side alleys. There were plenty of people around. In the middle of the terrace was a row of brand-new shops. Women with carrier bags stood round talking and one or two old men propped doors open, sucking on cigarettes. Julius would never go for him here anyway. It was too public.

It was easy finding the house Mary had mentioned. The whole terrace had been smartened up, like the ones in the exhibition – refurbished, that was the posh word they always used. Bathrooms had been put in, rewiring and painting done, and all the front doors painted the same slate-blue colour. Smack in the middle was the knocked-together house. He could see where a front door had been taken out and extra windows added instead. The door was shut and so were most of the curtains. Old chip papers and squashed Coke cans eddied round the front step and clattered in the gutter.

Stan found a low wall opposite, just up from the house, edging a brick-filled space where something had been demolished. His feet felt numb. Loosening the laces of Jack's boots he wiggled his toes about, then he straightened up and stared across at the house.

He was there a long time, just leaning against the wall, while the shops emptied and filled up again. A motor bike cannoned down the street with an earsplitting roar and the old men cursed it. Then, in the middle of the street, some little kids started to do a kind of play; the girl with the pram had put pink, high-heeled shoes on and a boy was applying lipstick in crazy lines.

Suddenly the curtains of the knocked-together house were pulled back and somebody was rattling the door-knob from inside. Stan stood up and moved away from the wall. Then the slate-blue door opened and children spilled through on to the pavement, pushed out by a striped red buggy that contained a toddler muffled up in a blue pramsuit.

'Put our Kevin's bootees on, love,' a voice said to a small girl who'd squeezed out with the buggy. 'He'll have 'em off before we get to Ferris's but it's not warm. Sara and Katie, come back! We're getting your gran's potatoes first.'

The twin girls who'd run out first were already near the top of the street but they turned back when their mother shouted at them and started to walk back slowly, with tiny steps, avoiding the cracks in the pavement in case the bears got them.

The woman bending over the buggy was very young. Her face had been pretty once but there were already pulled-down lines in the cheeks and round the mouth that you only expected to see in much older people. She had a frizz of thick coarse hair dyed blonde. The baby had blond hair too, all curly. It could be me, Stan thought, sitting there in the buggy with my blue bootees on. Our Kevin. It could be me.

The child was still being got ready for the walk when the twins came back. They took their older sister's hand and everyone crossed the street together. The woman was promising to take them to the rec when they'd got Gran her potatoes. Her voice was kind.

It was not his mother. The Gleghorns had moved on years ago, if they'd ever been there. There were thou-sands of streets, and thousands of girls that got preg-nant. Old women mixed things up, Stan knew that. And yet he went on staring.

The young woman was very shabby and she was going along the street in blue bedroom slippers edged with nylon fur, and a long black coat with buttons missing, wrapped round her like a cloak. Underneath he could see a bit of a spotted overall.

They were going to Ferris's, a greengrocer's on its own, near the bottom of the street. The pavement was very uneven. Sara, skipping ahead, got the toe of her sandal stuck under a crack and went down howling. There was a bloody graze along her arm and the sight of it set Kevin off too. Everyone stopped. The girls guarded the buggy while Sara was gathered into her mother's arms and soothed down. The woman's voice was surprisingly soft and low. It didn't go with the slippers and the hard blonde hair. There were no words but it reminded Stan of the warm bubbling noise of the woodpigeons he could hear at night at the end of their street in London. She was so kind to Sara.

He gazed and gazed, unable to think or speak, or yet to move away, looking for something he could not put a name to. His body was tight with a terrible passion that had suddenly swelled up in him, choking him strangely, turning him to stone.

And he wanted to be Kevin in the buggy, and that this young girl should be his mother. He wanted to go to her and say, 'I'm Stan, I've run away. I'm yours. Love me.'

Then there was the rumble of a motor-bike engine a few streets off. When the woman heard it she turned her head and saw Stan staring. He looked harder, searching the face, but there was nothing there. She was not his mother and she never could have been. When he was born she could have only been about ten years old.

He was still standing by the wall when they came out of the shop, lugging the potatoes. All the children were sucking ice-lollies. They were laughing, on their way to Gran's, then to the rec. Stan saw himself start to walk slowly towards them.

Then the street exploded as the motor bike came roaring back in a shine of chrome and black leather. The children screamed and fell back on to the pavement in a frightened tangle of wiggly pink legs and someone rushed over to them, swearing loudly at the disappearing bike.

At last the woman settled everyone down again and Kevin was left proudly clutching the pack of potatoes on his blue lap. Once again they all got ready to cross the street. As she walked past him Stan put his hand out and touched the black coat gently.

Chapter Ten

Vera came back at eight o'clock that night. She made a pot of tea and settled herself by the fire with Stan next to her, uncomfortable on an upright dining-chair with a scratchy horsehair seat. He got ready for another interrogation, and made a pretence of drinking the tea. It was much too strong for him and there was no sugar. But he didn't dare say anything; this woman rather frightened him.

'I'll be straight with you,' she said. 'I went to see Harry Andrews after my meeting, I've known him all his life. He was one of my pupils. Bright enough boy, though not university material. He's a police officer.'

Stan's heart flipped over and he turned hopeless eyes on her. He'd ruffled up his hair again so that it resembled an untidy nest and he'd put the old spectacles in his pocket, just hoping she wouldn't look at him too closely and ask a load of questions.

'I decided to ask his advice about you but he wasn't there. He's up in Newcastle on some job or other, back late tomorrow morning they told me. We'll go then.'

Willis, Harry Andrews' deputy, knew Vera Stott too; most people did round here. The funny thing was he'd already had a man in about this boy, a lorry-driver who'd picked him up in the Midlands. Someone had phoned him up apparently, asking a lot of questions and saying he was the boy's father. This truck-driver, Jack Brierley, had said he thought the police should know, that he felt 'uneasy' about it.

So when Vera Stott had turned up, talking about what sounded like the same lad, Willis had really started to wonder what was going on. There were no reports in on a boy fitting the description but he'd only just come on duty and he'd not checked with headquarters. He nearly mentioned Jack Brierley's visit but he'd thought better of it. Vera Stott may be the leading light of the local Sally Army but it didn't mean she had access to confidential information, and the lorry-driver's business was private, like hers.

There she stood, stiff as a post on the other side of the desk, unsmiling, formidable and hard, in her straw bonnet. She still looked just as she did twenty years ago when she was waiting for the delivery of the twelve times table. She'd been his first class teacher at the grammar school; Harry wasn't the only one who'd suffered.

Unless something came in that night the boss could deal with her himself. Willis had merely written a memo and put it in his in-tray.

Vera told Stan he could sleep in the front room, 'the parlour' she called it though it felt more like a museum, and there was a faint smell of gas. As he made the pillows and rugs she'd given him into a bed, on the settee, he could hear her bumping about upstairs.

He went into the tiny scullery to help Mary wash the cups; she may be getting a bit weak in the head but at least she wasn't suspicious of him. 'Our Vera's stopping tonight,' she told him apologetically, 'for company like.'

Because of me, Stan thought. Well, he could hardly blame them. Anyone else would have had him down to that police station in five minutes flat, after hearing how he'd pushed his way into the house. But Vera had talked to the 'Army' about it apparently, and they'd prayed for Stan, and for wisdom, all together. He'd got that to thank for the fact that he was still free.

The word 'police' threatened him though. The more he thought about it the more certain he was that he shouldn't stick around to see what happened; it was just asking for trouble. He'd got himself this far and although Warrington wasn't Dublin it was a sight nearer to Ireland and freedom than Auntie Marjorie's. He'd be chucking his luck away if he stayed here, only to be carted back to London.

When she came downstairs again Vera decreed that they'd have a look at the television and she put her glasses on, to read the *Radio Times*. 'I don't look at it much mesel', Georgie,' Mary had confided to him in the scullery. 'I can't see it too well. I like the wireless, me. Our Vera views though. She watches the news, and them documentaries.'

'Should I make the fire up?' Stan asked Vera nervously. It had been made clear to him that he was expected to view too, perched on that horsehair dining-chair.

'You could do,' she said, quite kindly. Then she sharpened again. 'Don't go putting too much on though. We can't afford to waste it, not at that price.'

He bent over the grate, poking and rearranging the cobbles of coal with a pair of brass tongs, then shovelling slack on. He carefully swept the porridge-coloured tiles with a half-hairless brush, then took up his position on the hard chair, between the two old ladies.

Vera sat dead opposite the TV set, then she leant past him and switched it on. 'There's a medical programme I want to see,' she announced. 'And we can watch the ten o'clock news. I don't think there's very much else. Do you like television?'

'Sometimes,' Stan muttered. 'Some of the programmes. I like the wildlife ones.'

It didn't matter what you liked at Auntie Marjorie's, the machine never went off; and Kingsley McCann was the original TV kid. Sometimes Stan tried to do his home-

100

work up in the bedroom but it was freezing in there, and there was nothing to write on except your knee. But it was impossible doing anything downstairs with the telly, and they always had it so loud. When he was doing something like Maths he sometimes asked for it to be switched off, but as soon as Auntie Marjorie was out of the way Kingsley always turned it on again and plonked himself in front of it, defying Stan to object with that pathetic little grin that made him want to commit murder.

'There's some serials I do like, Georgie . . .' Mary was saying, but the music was playing for Vera's programme. '*Husht,*' she ordered her, turning the sound up. She appeared to be rather deaf in one ear and she sat sideways on to the set, hunched right over it.

The programme was about death in childhood in northern cities and a special five-year survey someone had carried out in Sheffield. The camera cut from rows of howling babies to a bespectacled paediatrician called Edward Gomme.

'Little Teddy Gomme, Mary,' Vera shouted over the commentary. 'Do you remember him? I used to teach him at Greenford Avenue. Brilliant boy, he was.'

She huddled nearer to the screen, oblivious of the nodding older sister and of the silent rigid Stan who had eyes for nothing but the creeping hands of the electric clock over the sideboard. If he got away now he could catch a train to Liverpool from Central Station. There was a night crossing, he remembered that from the travel poster, and with a bit of luck he'd make it. He felt safer travelling in the dark, and it was madness to stay here any longer. He stood up, and went to the door.

Vera noticed. 'Where are you off to?' she said.

'Just got to go to the lavatory – I'll be down in a minute.'

She nodded and went back to little Teddy Gomme

who was now in full view, turning over a screaming baby on a table.

'Put the bathroom heater on for me, chuck,' Mary whispered to him. 'I'll not be long out of bed, it's that parky.'

Stan went up the stairs slowly, deliberately clomping with his boots. At the top he opened the bathroom door, put the heater on then shut it again with a bang. Then, quietly as he could manage, he slipped downstairs again and into the front parlour.

It would have to be a window. The front door was swollen with damp against two rusty bolts and hadn't been opened in years. Old Mary had told him that. And to get to the back and out through the yard meant passing the dragon on guard by the television set. The parlour window could be got open though, with a bit of fiddling. Nails had been driven into the frame on each side, to stop an intruder sliding it up from the street, but he could probably work them loose.

He looked round the cold dingy little room and his eyes came to rest on the copper kettle. That wad of notes rolled up and secured with a rubber band was pretty fat. With that in his pocket his troubles would be over, money troubles, anyhow. He wouldn't need to worry about where his next meal was coming from, or buying his ticket to Liverpool and on the ferry.

It was terrible, but he'd have to borrow it. *Borrow*, not steal. Once he was on the boat he'd find a quiet, private corner and count it all, then he'd make a note of the amount in his Woolies' diary. One day he'd make it up to Mary, just like he was going to make it up to Elspeth, go back and rescue her from Kingsley. But first, to explain why he couldn't stay, he was going to write her a letter, to read when he'd gone.

'It's right comfy that little settee is, Georgie,' someone said behind him, and Stan spun round. Mary was standing in the doorway, peering in at him with a blue hot-water bottle under her arm. He jumped, snatched his fingers away from the knob of the copper kettle and looked at her. 'You off to bed then?' he said.

'I am that, I don't keep late nights, me. Our Vera's still viewing.'

'Come and watch the news,' the sister's thin high voice rapped from the back room. 'Young people aren't properly informed these days, even though television and radio offer it all to them on a plate. It makes for lazy minds in my opinion, but there it is. Hurry up, I'm not keeping this door open.'

'Good-night, Mary,' he whispered as the old bent figure made its slow way up the stairs; then he went along the cold passage obediently and resumed his seat on the hard little chair.

The first few minutes of the news were a nightmare. What if they were still carrying the drugs story? A racket 'nationwide' the newspaper had said. What if they flashed photos up on the screen, asking for help from the general public? What if they flashed *him* up? Every time there was a change of subject Stan stiffened, and closed his eyes. But half-way through there was a news flash about a major air disaster. A plane full of holiday-makers, homebound from the Costa del Sol, had crashed into the sea only minutes after take-off, and there were no survivors. The bulletin was extended to allow for telephone numbers so that worried relatives could phone in.

Stan let the grisly facts and figures wash over him, sagging inwardly with relief. There'd be no time for anything about his story now, not even if it was scheduled. He'd escaped Vera finding him out because two hundred and fifty innocent people had died.

Perhaps it was an example of the fact that 'All things work together for good', that peculiar quotation from the Bible embroidered and hung in a frame over Mary's mantelpiece. If it was Stan didn't like it very much; he couldn't believe in a God like that.

The minute the news programme was over Vera snapped it off and got to her feet. 'Bed,' she said. 'I can't keep very late nights these days.' 'Bed' obviously meant he was expected to go too. 'I'll just lock up,' she told him, and she went through to the scullery, sliding bolts home and turning the large key in the heavy old kitchen door. When she came back he saw her put it in her pocket. That was one way of escape written off anyway.

'I'll say good-night then,' she told him, glancing into the cold gassy parlour before climbing the stairs. 'I hope you sleep. We'll go and have a word with Harry Andrews in the morning.'

Not if I have anything to do with it, Stan was thinking, trying to get comfortable on the narrow settee. He was much too long for it and his feet stuck out over the side; it smelt of mothballs too, like everything else in the house. He listened to the noises overhead for a bit, a door opening then the lavatory flushing, then another door. When there'd been quiet for five minutes he got out of his blankets and crept across the room to the heavy bookcase under the window. Before Vera had switched the light off he'd noticed something that was going to be useful to him.

It was an *A-Z* of Liverpool in street maps, falling to pieces and with 'Vera Stott' inked on the front page. Stan could just read it by the light of the street lamp outside. She'd probably bought it when she became a student at the university. OK, it was years old and they'd probably pulled most of Liverpool down by now, but they couldn't have moved the sea. The docks would still be in the same place and the main station too, with luck. Stan was good at map-reading and he found it easily, a black oblong marked 'Lime Street' in the middle of a tangle of railway lines. It didn't look much of a walk from there to the docks and once he'd found them he could ask someone where the Dublin boats sailed from.

He thought of tearing the page out and keeping it but it didn't feel right. Somehow it was worse than nicking that food from the supermarket. Perhaps it was because of the name written in the front. He could just see the young Vera Stott pedalling about on a sit-up-and-beg bicycle with a basket full of books, that keen clever face staring straight ahead determinedly, going too fast for the boys to keep up. The old *A–Z* was part of her history. He climbed into his blankets with it and shone his torch on to Lime Street Station. He could memorize it easily, or else copy it in to the back of his notebook . . .

At last his feet were warming up and he'd started to feel drowsy. It was probably the gassy smell; they ought to get it seen to. Slowly the grid of Liverpool streets started to wiggle and blur under his eyes. Getting going didn't seem such an issue any more. He was safe here, nobody was trying to get at him and Vera was already snoring loudly in the room over his head. Within five minutes, unable to stop himself, Stan was gently snoring too.

He woke up hours later with an agonizing pain in his back; he'd had to fold himself up like a jack-knife to fit on to that settee and it had given him cramp. He'd got no watch and the old clock on the mantelpiece hadn't worked in years but it was light outside. Nobody was about though, from the sound of things, and Vera was still snoring away up above. He grinned and swung his legs out of the blankets. You'd expect a woman like that to be an early riser. Perhaps it was earlier than it felt.

It didn't take him long to get ready. He'd slept in his clothes and there was no way he could wash, or clean his teeth. He had one last look at the map of central Liverpool before putting the book back in its place; then he pulled his boots on.

In the end he left most of Mary's money, peeling off just three of the notes and shoving the rest back. He hated himself for taking any. As he folded the bills and pushed them into the pocket of his trousers, he tried not to think of that innocent trusting face, of the glee with which the old woman had clipped his hair, of the fact that he was Georgie.

He couldn't leave a note either. Sister Vera didn't know about the secret cache of money in the copper kettle and she'd shout at Mary for her stupidity, if she once found out.

I'm sorry, he said to himself as he picked at the two rusty nails till he could prise them out of the window frame, I'm sorry, Mary. I'll pay it all back, in time.

There would be time for paying back everything, her savings, the food from Mike's supermarket; there'd be time for everything one day. But he'd got to concentrate on getting to Ireland first, and finding Sid.

He eased the window up, climbed through into the deserted street and started walking. Behind him, Mary's little house slept quietly on in the early morning.

Chapter Eleven

Warrington to Liverpool was a cinch, compared with the rest of his journey. He had a long cold wait for a train on a windy platform with rain trickling down his neck, but at least no one had come up and started firing questions at him, not even the man in the ticket office where he'd asked for half fare.

That had been a risk in itself. The last few times he'd been to the cinema they'd asked him how old he was, before letting him in with Kingsley, at child's rate. But he'd got to make Mary's money last: he was only fourteen anyhow, even if he did look older.

The train rattled along quite quickly for most of the journey. Stan turned his face to the window as soon as he got in and kept it turned; open railway carriages were like compartments on the London Underground, places where you got stared at because people had nothing better to do. Stan didn't want to be stared at; he still felt nervous about that picture they'd printed in the paper. Most of the people in the carriage had newspapers and how did he know that they weren't still running the drugs story? He stared through old Jack's spectacles at the cluttered grey-green landscape as it swung past the window. The sooner he could get off and find somewhere quiet to wait till it was time to go for the evening boat the better. He was starting to hate enclosed spaces.

Lime Street was like any other big railway station, echoey and vast with a metallic, sexless voice giving out incomprehensible announcements over a tannoy. 'What's she say, mate?' an old man asked him, marooned with a tatty blue duffel bag in the middle of a vast tiled floor. 'I can never understand them things. I'm trying to get to Lytham St Anne's and I've missed one train.'

'Dunno,' Stan muttered, moving off. 'Sorry, I'm in a hurry myself.' He wasn't in a hurry at all, he'd got hours to kill, but a small dark figure lounging against a telephone kiosk had struck terror into him, just for a second. Only when the man had thrown his cigarette away and walked past him across the main concourse had Stan got a proper look. The poor man wouldn't win any beauty competitions; his face looked as if it had been moulded from Plasticene, then flung against a wall, but at least he didn't resemble a rat.

On the train he'd wondered whether to wander round Liverpool for an hour or two. It was a place he always felt he'd known about, because of the Beatles. They seemed like history now, especially since that nutter in New York had shot John Lennon. Stan felt sad when they played old Beatles numbers on the radio. Why kill a pop singer? It was pointless.

The city was always in the news these days because it had gone bankrupt or something. Vera Stott couldn't be too pleased about that, Liverpool was her university. The people didn't exactly look bankrupt though, rushing off to catch trains with their big posh suitcases. Everyone was in a hurry, trundling rapidly across the pale shiny tiles as if they were on wheels. Nobody bothered about Stan. They were all much too busy getting to their offices or going to interviews, or meeting up with friends for a coffee.

He should have been grateful. He'd been trying to keep a low profile since leaving London and every time anyone came anywhere near him, looking as if they might speak, he felt slightly sick. But the crowds and the rush filled him with an unutterable loneliness. Everyone here belonged to somebody. That morning they'd come out from a place that was home and, when their work was over, they'd go back to it, drawn by invisible cords. It was like that hymn Auntie Marjorie was so fond of, 'He drew me with the cords of love', that's what it said.

Stan hadn't understood about 'the cords' till they'd taken Mrs Kelly into hospital and ended the good time in the flat with him and Sid. Nothing had felt right since then, or settled, or permanent. He wanted to find those cords again, to take them in his hands and be happy. That was really why he was going to Ireland. Sid was part of the good time, and farmer Joe was too because he was all that was left of Mrs Kelly.

Stan wished somebody would come along and give him an injection, knock him out and wake him up again when it was time to get on the boat. Too many hours stretched ahead of him and he didn't want to spend them wandering round Liverpool. It wasn't fear of Julius, he'd obviously thrown him off by now. It was an unexpected inner weariness that had come over him quite suddenly, out of the blue. Instead of feeling bullish because he was in a stone's throw of Liverpool Docks, Stan actually felt like crying. It was as if he'd got caught up in a time warp and become a toddler again. Part of him wanted to take hold of someone else's hand and be looked after; a tiny part wanted to go back to London, to the old familiar life. None of him wanted to get on that boat to Dublin, yet it was there for the taking. He'd even seen seagulls waddling about on the station concourse. That's how near the sea was.

He swung his rucksack up on his back again, went into the Gents and had a good wash, then he spent a long time cleaning his teeth. Doing it made him think of Kingsley. He never cleaned his so they always looked as if they were covered with yellow slime. He swished the water round the basin and spat vigorously. Kingsley would have his mother to himself now; Elspeth didn't count.

Elspeth. He wasn't going to let himself think about her, or about old, bewildered Mary waking up and being told that Georgie had vanished. All that was on the high dark shelf in his mind. He ran his tongue round his teeth and sucked in the minty taste. Getting cleaned up had made him feel a bit better. Breakfast. That was the next move.

From the station entrance he could see a McDonald's. He crossed the road, went in and ordered the works, gobbling it down like a pig. Only when the food hit his stomach did he realize how long he'd gone without food. Since Mary's Lancashire hot-pot he'd only had a small supper of cheese and biscuits. Vera ate sparingly.

He hung around in the café as long as he could, buying a second large Coke and drinking it very slowly. But when a girl wiping tables came round to his seat for the third time and waved a wet cloth aggressively under his nose, Stan took the hint. There wasn't any law, surely, about hanging round in places like this, so long as you didn't make trouble, but he didn't want her pointing him out to the manager.

He swilled down his Coke, slung his rucksack on again and went back to the station. It was quieter now, with fewer people around, which was bad news for him. Anyone who worked there, cleaning the place up or selling things in the shops, might start wondering about a boy like him if he hung around for too long. He could always walk down to the docks and find out where the boat sailed from but something told him it would be too risky in broad daylight. Ferries and airports meant all kinds of officials standing round and there'd be police at this terminal too, because of the Belfast crossing.

Instead he studied the large city map, under glass in the main entrance hall. Liverpool may be bankrupt but it was obviously dead proud of itself. Underneath the grid of streets there was a long list of 'attractions' tourists

110

might wish to inspect; two famous cathedrals, one built in the shape of a wigwam, a great art gallery and the university on the hill that had produced Miss Vera Stott. The docks were 'attractions' too apparently and Stan examined them closely. The names sounded like London pubs, Kings, Queens and Coburg. 'Ferry terminal' a notice said in the middle of the map, next to something marked 'Royal Liver Building'. That was where he'd got to go, and it didn't look too far away. The map only showed the main roads but he was planning to avoid those. There'd be plenty of side-streets, particularly in a dock area, even in this 'splendid Victorian city'.

One thing on the list was a library and it looked very near. Libraries at least weren't stuffed with plain-clothes policemen, and nobody would bother with him if he spent an hour or so in there. It would be warm, too, with somewhere to sit down. But he'd got to have something to read. He couldn't get a book out without a ticket and he wasn't going to spend the time looking at newspapers. If they were full of drugs and missing-boy stories Stan just didn't want to know. So he went over to the main news stall and spent two of Mary's precious pounds on a paperback.

Ten minutes later he was comfortably installed in a large reading room. He'd found the City Library easily, followed the arrows and walked in. Nobody stopped him or asked him what he was doing. The man at the desk might have been a bit surprised though, if he'd seen what was in Stan's W. H. Smith's bag. The other people at his table were reading things like the *Financial Times* and the *Spectator*. He was glued to a bumper edition of *The Famous Five*, three stories in one.

He didn't like to think what Miss Dobbs would say, stuff like this was for little kids and he'd left it behind years ago. But plunging back into that safe, simple world of adventure, where everything came right in the end, was a strange comfort to him, the way he felt now, with a

111

great grey sea crashing about in his head, that sea he was soon to sail on, uncertain, towards an uncertain future.

Miss Dobbs was right though when she told them Enid Blyton was boring and repetitive and he started to feel drowsy. Very soon Anne, Dick and Julian blurred into a single three-headed monster with a wagging tail and a keeper in grey shorts called George. They were all off to Kirrin Island again where Uncle Quentin was conducting secret experiments in a horrible boarding school. After his uncomfortable night on Mary's settee Stan needed a bit of solid kip. Gradually his shorn head fell forward and he cradled it in his arms, sleeping like a baby.

When he woke up the chairs round him were empty and a man was clearing away all the newspapers. 'Finished with this, have you?' he said sarcastically, sweeping up the *Farmer's Weekly*. He'd seen the cover of Stan's book, Julian, Dick, George and Anne running down to the sea with Timmy romping ahead of them. His eyes met Stan's coldly. Mental pygmy, they were saying.

As he went out he looked up at the clock. Coming in here had killed a fair bit of time but it was still too early to risk going down to the docks. He'd passed a cinema on his way up from the station and they were showing *Back to the Future*. He'd seen it loads of times but it was one big laugh, and it'd be warm and dark inside. With luck he could sit through the programme twice and then it'd be time to go for the ferry. He located the cinema and walked in.

The little man behind the ticket desk looked hostile and Stan topped him by six inches. He didn't want to get into an argument about his age and child tickets. All his risks had paid off so far, getting himself here from Warrington on a public train, then going into McDonald's and the City Library, but he wasn't trusting his luck too far. Sooner or later somebody was going to cut up rough.

So he paid full price and settled himself down in an

almost empty cinema. It was a pity about the dim lighting. He'd woken up again now and he could have finished 'Five Have a Wonderful Time' before the film started.

After killing all those hours in the area of Lime Street Station Stan nearly missed the boat. He saw the entire programme through twice, though he slept a bit during the second showing, and every time the lights went up he glanced at the cinema clock. It was only when the ice-cream girl appeared in her spotlight for the third time, and he checked the time again, that he realized the clock must have stopped. It had been saying seven thirty-five for the last hour.

The street outside told him it was much later. The crowds were out, not office workers this time but people dressed for a night on the town. All the pavements were awash and McDonald's was obviously doing a roaring trade. It must be nine o'clock at least and his boat went in twenty minutes. He'd been planning to go back to Lime Street and have another look at the map but there was no time now; he'd just have to rely on the map in his head.

He remembered a street running parallel to the broad main road down to the docks and he located it now, behind the Information Centre. It was as he'd imagined it, and what he wanted, fairly narrow and ill-lit, not a place the night people would hang about in. He set off along it at a steady run, his thumbs through the straps of the rucksack, his head tucked in, relaxing slightly as the road began to slope downwards. It would meet the Mersey soon and that meant the sea.

He passed a shop boarded up with a clock sticking out over the street. The hands said ten past nine. A youth in a donkey jacket who didn't look much older than he was came up from the corner on an old bike, with a wobbly front light. 'Am I going in the right direction for the Irish ferries?' Stan shouted. It was the first time

113

he'd heard his own voice saying something that mattered for what felt like centuries, and it slightly unnerved him. *He was going to Ireland,* he'd as good as said it. Saying things made them real.

The boy stopped. 'Yes, mate. Carry on down here, first left, and you'll hit the docks.' Then he looked at his watch. 'You going for the nine-twenty then?'

Stan nodded.

'Cutting it fine, aren't you? They'll have finished loading by now.'

He must have looked crushed because the other boy stared at him sympathetically, then turned his bike round. 'Get on,' he said, 'it'll only take a minute on this. Put your bag in the basket.'

Stan stuffed the rucksack in, making the wickerwork creak. 'It's my mam's, this is,' the boy said. 'I've got a racer but I use this one for deliveries. I do the free newspaper on Thursdays. I've just finished . . . Are you right then? Hang on.'

Grunting with the extra weight he pedalled off slowly. Stan clutched at his shoulders as they bumped along, bewildered at the unexpected kindness. Why should a Liverpool paperboy go out of his way after an evening's work to get a stranger like him on to a boat on time? Julius apart he'd been dead lucky on this journey. Jack Brierley could easily have taken him to the police, so could Vera Stott, but for some reason people had stayed on his side.

He was obviously meant to go to Ireland and find Sid and Mrs Kelly's brother, and he wasn't on his own; he was daft to think that. As the streets started to slope away more sharply, down to the Mersey, his mood lightened and he gripped harder at the boy's anorak. He'd nearly made it. What was there to feel depressed about?

Quite suddenly the lowish houses gave way to much taller buildings that loomed over the two boys blackly as the old bike bumped on and off kerbs and cut through a tangle of little roads. Stan could see cars everywhere and a long line of vehicles edging slowly towards the low hump of a ship moored at the dockside, with more crawling over a clanking gangway. The ferry boat was in shadow but studded with lights from the inside and there were bigger lights from the sprawl of the terminal buildings alongside, winking into the water.

'That's your boat, mate,' the boy said, cutting nonchalantly across a jumble of access roads and past No Entry signs. 'I can't go any further. Got your ticket ready?'

'Er, well no. Didn't really have time to get one,' Stan grunted, clambering off the bike. He ought to kick himself, all those hours in Liverpool, simply waiting for the dark to come and protect him, and now they might not let him on because he hadn't bought the necessary.

'I'd try and get straight on then, if I were you. They'll give you one on the boat this time of year, business is pretty slack. The office is back there,' and the paperboy jerked his head back into the blackness of the dockside. 'You're too late for that really. They're loading the last few trucks. See you,' and he remounted the bike, whistling. 'So long then, mate.'

'So long,' Stan said, 'and thanks very much.'

He shouldered the rucksack and stumbled on weak legs down a chained-off walkway that led to the boat. There was still a small queue of people waiting to show their tickets, among them a group of noisy young men and women with enormous rucksacks and striped university scarves. If they actually let him on he'd stick with them, Stan decided. He could be taken for a student himself and he'd be a lot less conspicuous in a group.

He watched in fascination as the very last truck clanked into the bowels of the ferry. There were shouts and signals, then the jaws of the boat folded in on

115

themselves with a rusty jerking noise. The multi-coloured queue shuffled forwards.

A small man in front of him turned round and said pleasantly, in a thick Irish accent, 'Are you travelling alone then, son?'

'Yes. I'm going to see my brother, he's out there farming.'

'Well, it's a fine country surely. We've got some of the best land in Europe, and don't let anyone be telling you otherwise . . .'

But the man checking tickets cut him off officiously and he passed through obediently on to the boat.

'I . . . I didn't have time to go to the ticket office,' Stan whimpered, looking down at the outstretched hand, his insides snaking up and down quite violently. This was the crunch. If the official cut up rough and stuck to the rules and regulations, it'd be the end of his journey and the start of a lot more trouble. But the man merely looked along the remainder of the queue and muttered something sourly, under his breath. Then he fished out a printed pad from his back pocket and scribbled something on it.

'Coming back, are you?'

'I don't . . . what d'you mean?'

'Are you coming *back*? One way or return?'

'Oh. No, I'm staying over there. One way. Please. Here, I don't know the exact fare,' and Stan dumped Mary's banknotes into the waiting palm.

The official took what he wanted and pressed the change into Stan's hand with a spiteful twist. 'You could have checked, couldn't you? You could have gone to the proper place like everybody else. Go on, hop it. I could do without people like you on a night like this.' It was cold and starting to rain, and Stan could feel the boat sway under him as he stepped on board.

There were a couple more people behind him without tickets, bearded and with bulging rucksacks, making very polite apologies to the moody ticket-inspector in cultivated, far-back accents.

He signalled them impatiently on to the boat, resisting the urge to prod. 'Go on,' he said. 'The rest of your party has only just turned up. I could do without people like you.'

Stan grinned to himself when he heard that. The man obviously said it to everybody under twenty.

The last passenger to go aboard had already bought his ticket. Well, that was no surprise, the only surprise was that he hadn't gone over by air. The ferry official could smell money and this guy obviously had plenty of it; pale lightweight suit, silk shirt, dark tie, those tinted glasses the nobs always favoured. Quite a change from the rucksack brigade, making their row. He could smell hair lacquer as the man pushed past; the hair was black and very tightly curled, it looked almost like a perm.

Julius had reached Liverpool within two hours of losing Stan in the streets behind Central Station. He wasn't piddling about any more, playing cops and robbers with a kid. The boy was bound for Ireland via Liverpool. That thicko of a lorry-driver had let out the Liverpool bit on the phone, and it had got to be Ireland because it was where the big brother was; little brother had got a kind of crush on him, according to Victor. Silly little sod.

Victor hadn't been much help to him in the last few days, he'd been too busy 'helping the police', but the boys in Liverpool had, and every boat to leave this dump had been checked by one of them. Julius had done his share of watching too because Stan Mellor was his baby. He'd only gone off duty for a few hours to get new clothes and freshen up, then have the hair job done. They'd organized all that for him. Liverpool was quite a place really; pity it was going down the nick.

It was a stroke of luck that he'd been the one to close in. He'd just been leaning against the ticket office, having a quiet smoke and working up an appetite for dinner, when he'd spotted the boy, large as life, getting off a bike and running down the walkway towards the boat.

Julius laughed silently at Stan's pathetic attempts at disguise, the silly granny glasses and the chopped-about hair. He still had the rucksack though and the man's insides tightened. His fingers were tingling to get at it now.

He'd had a very long wait, and a cold one in this weather, but it was going to pay off richly. What was waiting anyhow? That was his game.

Chapter Twelve

Stan wanted to explore the ship. He'd never been on any kind of boat before, unless you counted those crazy dinghies you can propel round duckponds with your feet. Auntie Marjorie had taken him and Kingsley on one of those once, at a fair.

But now he was actually on board a great weakness overcame him, and he needed somewhere to sit down. His heart was whispering to him, 'I've done it, I'm free. *Alleluia!*' And he wanted to shout it out loud, so everyone could hear.

The boat moved slowly away from the pier in complete silence. It was marvellous. Men doing things with chains and winches, yellowy-orange in the artificial lights, stopped momentarily and looked up as the strip of water widened. One touched his cap as if some great personage had just passed by.

Some of the passengers leaned over the side and waved, and Stan waved with them. He felt he could stay there for ever, looking down into the dark thresh of the waves, at the greedy gulls following the boat in a tumble of wings.

But the crossing promised to be a bad one, the wind was up and it felt as if the water was getting choppy even here, away from the open sea. As they moved away from the dockside in the mist, the dazzle of the quayside lights was gradually swallowed up into an orange fuzz.

'Got your paper bag ready, have you?' one of the

students called out cheerfully. 'Feels as if it's going to be rough tonight.'

Stan smiled but said nothing. He didn't want to get into a conversation with anybody, or sit in any one place too long. They sold newspapers on the boat.

'Got a cabin?' the boy said. Stan shook his head. 'Neither have we, but there's plenty of room to stretch out, in the saloon. You don't really need one, this time of year. Waste of money.'

The boat was already swaying. Stan didn't know if he was going to be seasick or not. So far he felt fine and when a voice on the tannoy announced that you could get dinner in the restaurant, he suddenly realized he was famished again. It was hours since McDonald's.

He followed signs down on to B deck and after a few false turns located the self-service cafeteria. It wasn't busy, the whole boat seemed to be an acreage of empty seats and clean ashtrays. There were a few families with young children, one or two solitary men and the gang of students. Everyone else seemed to be a lorry-driver or a member of the crew.

'Of course, it's the time of the year,' he heard a man say to his wife. 'I suppose nearly everyone's back at work now. The cardeck's jammed with juggernauts and ten-ton trucks. Getting the car out'll be a bit tricky.'

Stan quite fancied having a look down below where all the lorries were parked, but a notice on the hatchway said 'Car-Drivers Only'. He didn't want to draw attention to himself by trespassing, not when he'd got as far as this with no questions asked.

In the cafeteria he threw caution away and bought a trayful of food, steak pie and potatoes, carrots and peas, apple tart and ice-cream, and a big mug of coffee. There wasn't much money left, when he'd paid for it all, but there'd be enough to make the phone call to Sid. When he got to Dublin he planned to get the number and phone from there. Then he'd have to wait around till somebody could come for him. He didn't have the proper address but the name of the town would do, and Joe Kelly's name. He wasn't going to think any further ahead than that, or wonder whether Vera's suspicions were right, that he wouldn't be all that welcome. One step at a time, that was his motto from now on.

He was still eating his apple tart when he noticed several people get up and make for the doorway. The boat was rocking and through a porthole he could see a dark, up-ended smudge that was the horizon.

'No sea-legs, some of 'em,' an oldish man in a boiler suit said, to nobody in particular, spearing a sausage. 'When you've done this run as long as I have your stomach's got itself a tin lining.' He grinned and washed the sausage down with tea.

Stan wanted to know how long it would be before they got to Dublin. He knew it was quite a long crossing. He opened his mouth to ask, then shut it again suddenly. There would be questions, curious looks, and perhaps someone sitting idly by would be listening, someone who'd seen that front-page spread in the London paper. He took his tray back to the hatch and decided to go up on deck.

He climbed as far as you could go, to a small upper deck with white steps leading on to it. These were chained off and a spotlight shone on the 'No Admittance' sign. Up above he could see an enclosed look-out, brightly lit inside, and there were two navy-blue figures in it slashed with gold braid, leaning over banks of dials. The rain was thickening now and he noticed that the cabin had little windscreen-wipers like a car.

He pulled his anorak hood on and fastened the strings, shoving the spectacles down into his trouser pocket. For the moment he could do without them, there was nobody about but him. Then one of the crew burst out of a doorway and ran past him, along the deck. 'Plenty of room inside, sir, there's nothing much to see out here, and you'll get soaked.'

Sir. Stan was tickled to death. 'Just getting a bit of fresh air,' he called, but the man had scuttled inside already.

He took the rucksack off and nudged it against the side of the deck with his boot. Then he leaned over the side and stared down, mesmerized by the speeding water lit up in orange and silver flashes by the lights from the boat as it sliced through the black chop of the waves. He loved the wildness, the din of bird cry, sea and wind.

Then a voice plucked him back from the edge of his dream. 'Mine, I think?' and someone was pushing at the rucksack with a small neat shoe. Stan had his body over it at once, instinctively, cradling it as if it were a small child, with his hands through the straps. Then he looked up.

'I come a long way for this, boyo. You put me to a lot of trouble, *see!*' Julius bunched his fist and rammed it under the boy's chin, driving his teeth together. Stan could have knocked him flying with a straight left, but he'd got both hands round the rucksack.

'I've had a lot of hard driving and waiting around, *see!* So have a lot of other people. *See!*' The fist came again. 'And I don't v̬ ᵤnt to wait any more, sonny boy, so where is it?'

'Where's what?' Stan's eyes glazed over and he braced himself against the side of the ship, steadying himself. He was good at waiting too.

'You *know*, you bloody *know*. The packet, from Victor. It's in there, isn't it? Now bloody give it to me or I'll get the police on to you. They'll soon sort you out.'

Stan heard himself laugh out loud. '*Police!* That's a laugh. Try pulling the other one. Fat chance you'd get I've seen the papers.'

Julius stared at him and a small silence fell on them both like a solitary pencil of light, seeking them out and folding them up in quietness, away from the noise of the sea and the howling rain. Ratface didn't look so cocky now. His smart clothes were sodden and crumpled and the fancy hairdo was coming out. Hs voice had changed slightly, it was almost pleading.

'Aw, c'mon, Stanley. Let me have it and I'll leave you alone. There'll be nobody after you, honest.'

'No, you're right there,' Stan said daringly, panic making him light-headed. 'But that's because there's nobody left. They're all in the clink now, aren't they? That's where you'll be soon. Hope you never come out,' he added.

Julius was thinking rapidly. The net of his underworld was spread wide. As well as his contacts in Liverpool, there were old enemies too, waiting their chance. Somebody else might have been on to the boy already, and made him an offer. Perhaps there was someone on this boat waiting to meet up with him. *Had he got to Stan soon enough?*

'I'll make it worth your while, Stanley boy. Five hundred, look, I'll give you five hundred over what anyone else has offered. C'mon,' he wheedled. 'Give us a break. You're out of your depth, boyo.'

Stan shook his head and said nothing. It would have been so easy to hand over the packet. Almost certainly, then, the man would leave him alone. Why didn't he just let him have it? Julius had already taken a wallet out and was fanning ten-pound notes in Stan's direction. The wind tore at them greedily.

He saw himself on the dark, rain-soaked deck, still hugging the rucksack, and shaking his head violently, as if it was all some weird nightmare, and he was outside his own body, just a ghost looking in. He didn't understand himself, or know where this sudden pig-headed resolve had come from, or why he was refusing to hand over Julius's filthy packet. It would be so easy.

Suddenly Ratface went for his legs and Stan crashed

over on to the deck. They rolled over and over, tangled up together, then the small man jammed his legs under a seat and got on top of him, scrabbling at the buckles on the rucksack. Stan twisted and pulled violently and managed to get free, still holding on to it by one strap.

Julius dived at him again, hooking an arm round his throat and pulling back against his shoulders, squeezing out the breath. With his free hand Stan grappled to escape, prising helplessly at the hard muscles that now locked him in, threatening to choke him. The man was very small but very powerful and now he was kicking savagely from behind, trying to bring him down again.

'OK.' Stan tried to speak but could only groan. Julius relaxed slightly; so his break was coming. He hadn't expected the rotten bloody little twister to put up a show like this, but Victor had always loathed him, clever type he always said, never missed a trick. Too clever by half, that one.

But in that second Stan got free and swung round to face him, the canvas satchel still dangling by a single strap.

'OK. You've had your fun, boyo. Give me what I came for, will you, now *gimme*!' The man went for him again but Stan heard himself half-shout, half-sob, 'Leave me *alone*! You're a nutter, Julius, you're off your rocker. D'you know that? Why can't you just leave me *alone*!' and then, 'Help me somebody, please *Help Me*!' to the deserted deck. And suddenly, in a great arc, his arm rose up slowly and he flung the rucksack over the side, far far out, into the boiling black sea.

Julius gasped. His eyes followed Stan's arm back to his side again, then dropped to the deck, unable to believe what he'd just seen. Then he cried out, a long anguished cry of real pain and loss, the sobbing of a miser for his lost gold.

Stan had never seen a man weep before but Ratface

was weeping now, and he lifted his arms up wildly to the sky then beat them deliriously on his knees, his thin body shaking convulsively, all doubled-up like a child in a fit of rage.

Then he went mad.

As he came at Stan the boy saw a knife in his hand. Now the rucksack had gone he could concentrate properly, and take advantage of his greater height and weight. But Julius was amazingly strong. Stan had got him by the wrist and was trying to twist the knife away, down towards the boards of the deck, but the man was too clever. The blade glittered, wavering slightly, but upright enough and moving only as he made it move, as he forced it down slowly, towards Stan's chest. Then he kneed him hard in the groin, and the boy crumpled on deck, with a groan.

Julius stood over him, knowing he was in control now, taking his time, but for Stan there seemed to be no time any more. As the boy stared up he was no longer looking at a person at all, but in the space where Julius's face had been there passed an unending procession of faces. He saw people who'd been kind to him and people who hadn't cared, people who'd begun to love him and then gone away. Hard dark memories all hopelessly jumbled up with the better things, with people smiling.

The knife was very near him now. Julius could drive it home then throw him into the sea, and nobody would ever find out. He was going to die. He was going through his life like people are supposed to do, when they are drowning.

So many faces, Auntie Marjorie's thin lips pressed tight against the occasional trembling that gave her away. The lovely Miss Dobbs and next to her his mother, the empty outline of a face with nothing in the middle to say who it was. He heard voices too, all the children in the homes and the special centres, the soft Irish voice of old Mrs Kelly mixed up with the whining bleat of Kingsley McCann.

Then a scream cut through it all, his own voice, high with terror, screaming above the bird cry and the thresh of the sea, and he felt his body rolling over and jerking loose as Julius suddenly lost his hold. Then he was standing upright on the deck.

'Hang on, mate,' somebody was saying. 'I had my eye on him in the bar. Nasty type. What's he been trying to do to you, for God's sake? Good job I came up here for a breather. I'll get help.' And he saw the little Irish man who'd spoken to him in the queue climb the ladder to the upper deck.

But then two men burst out from a hatchway behind Julius. They'd heard Stan cry out and had seen the struggle through a glass door. One of them was trying to get Julius by the shoulders while the other grabbed at the knife. Julius twisted away and someone screamed out. Then Stan saw blood splat down on the deck and a man sagged on to his knees. From the door near the steps a small string of onlookers was emerging, but still Julius fought to escape.

Stan turned and made off. There were no eyes for him while such a drama was going on. He spotted a door marked 'Crew Only', opened it, and saw steps. Gambling that he would meet nobody he slithered down them and through another door, then down more steps. He was in the engine room and the noise was deafening. At the far end someone with sleeves rolled up was hunched over dials. Stan turned back. They mustn't see him now. When Julius was banged up somewhere they'd start looking for him.

He stood at the bottom of the steps again, starting to panic. Then he heard shouts and a hubbub of voices overhead. His instinct was to go down another flight, but not back into the engine room. Instead he turned left through a door marked 'Cabins – First Class Only' and

ran down a line of closed doors. There were voices coming from the end but he shot past. More steps and a
painted hand that said 'Cars – No Entry During Crossing'.

Seconds later he was inching his way along the floor
of the cardeck, half-suffocated by the fug of oil and petrol
fumes, weaving in and out of gigantic wheels. The boat
was rocking violently. In the darkness Stan could feel
the huge trucks strain at their moorings.

In the din of the place he prayed that all the brakes
would stay good, and crept on towards the centre of the
hold.

Chapter Thirteen

When the men reached the cardeck Stan reckoned he must have got to the middle, but if they crawled under the lorries with their flashlights it would be all over. They only had to turn the beam up and they'd spot him, hanging from the underside of a great truck. His hands were thrust into what felt like huge iron sockets, his feet braced against an iron bar that ran across the vehicle in front of the middle wheels.

There were so many noises. The wild sea boomed under his head, the sound turning into gigantic gongs in the iron belly of the ship. Trucks squeaked and rattled all around him and there were muffled clankings whenever the boat went over hard. His own truck felt firm but he was terrified that everything would suddenly give way and something would roll back over him.

He was feeling horribly sick now. He dropped to the floor and vomited, hoping the sounds of the engines would drown the retching noise, praying that the smell wouldn't reach them.

There were two men.

'Don't reckon he could have got this far, unless he went through the engine room,' a voice said, 'and Bill was on duty down there. He didn't see anything.'

'What we supposed to be doing then?'

'I told you, check over this lot. You start at that end.'

'Y'mean, go right *underneath*?'

'Ye-es, well, as far as we can get like. That's what

Jackson said to me. The police'll be on when we get in, of course. He meant just check round generally.'

'We'll be late off then?'

'Suppose so. They won't be taking any chances. Mind you, it's the man they'll be interested in.'

They split up. Stan opened his eyes and saw the beams of light dipping and wavering on the whitish boards. He heard laboured breathing and caught sight of a navy-blue trouser-leg.

'Phew! Someone's been sick down here. Filthy pig. There are lavatories on B deck.'

'Plenty of sea available.' The older voice laughed.

'D'you reckon that's where he's gone then, this boy? D'you reckon he's swum for it?'

'Don't be bloody ridiculous. In the dead of night? As far out as this? We're not even in the lough yet. He'll only've jumped if he wants to commit suicide.'

'Wonder where he is then?'

'Dunno. They'll find him, when we dock. They won't let this lot off till they've been through everything.'

There was another silence and the beams flitted away downship. Then he heard shouting.

'OK, Phil. That's all we can do down here. We can't get under some of them. He couldn't be down here any-way, couldn't have made it in the time. Damned fool's errand this is, if you ask me. We'll do the Gents next. Are you right, then?'

The heavy door thumped to and there was a rattle as they locked it from the other side. Stan began slithering in and out of the gigantic wheels till at last he reached the side of the ship.

He straightened up very gingerly, because his legs were threatening to crumple under him. When his head had slowed down to a gentle spin he checked on each of the exit doors. There were four of them, all locked. So he was a prisoner.

His best bet was to go back the way he'd come and climb

129

up into the bowels of one of the trucks, tuck himself away from the wheels and moving parts and, when the lorry moved forward off the boat, go off with it, crucified horizontally, bumping unseen and glorious into the free Dublin air.

But Stan knew he couldn't do it. His torch had gone with his rucksack to the bottom of the sea. However carefully he checked over the trucks he could only position himself by feel and he might easily pick on the wrong place, get caught up in some moving part when the engine started and end up in little pieces, all minced up like Peter Blackley's dad who fell into a cutting-machine at his factory and died. He daren't risk it.

So he went to the back of the ship, remembering something the lovely Miss Dobbs had once told them. She'd said, 'Remember that the teacher's pencil's always at its sharpest at the beginning of the day,' and it would be true of the police too. By the time they got to this lot they'd have checked more than a hundred vehicles and they'd be sick and tired of it. There was just a chance they might not be so thorough at the end. He'd have to take it.

There were only a few lorries you could actually get into. Most were new and securely locked and bolted. A handful had tarpaulins to climb under, just two were more solid with canvas doors tied together at the back with rope. Stan examined them both. The first was filled with wooden crates, there would be room for a boy to slip down in between them and get out of sight; but they were too tightly fitted in and, anyway, he couldn't budge them an inch.

He fastened the tarpaulins together again and climbed into the other one. It was half-filled with boxes that probably contained tinned food. The arrangement was haphazard. The cartons weren't neatly stacked but heaped up in one corner in a rough pyramid. Stan lugged them away from the lorry wall and made a space big enough to get down and curl up on the floor. Then he rebuilt the outside of the pyramid leaving a couple of cartons on the top, half overlapping the entrance-hole. He tied up the canvas doors from inside as well as he could, then climbed down inside the boxes and pulled the two top ones over the hole from underneath, working them into place with sore fingers.

It was very warm and the darkness was total. Through the slit he'd left for air came the smell of cardboard and diesel oil. Soon he began to feel drowsy. The sea felt as if it had flattened out a bit and the engine noises had changed; they sounded lower now, more grinding. The boat must be coming into Dublin.

'Don't let them find me,' Stan said to himself, over and over again, 'I'm so near now. Please don't let them,' and in the dark warm fug of the boxes he drifted into unconsciousness.

'How much longer are they going to be? What the hell –'

'I'd put that fag out, mate, you can see the notices.'

'Ah, fer God's sake.'

'Well, they'll be none too sweet, having to go over this lot. Don't want to slow the thing up any more, do you? I can't stick all this hanging around. We're hours late as it is.'

Stan woke to the same heavy darkness but he could now feel cold air. He moved two boxes apart and got a split of light. There were seagulls crying, and the rumble of wheels over a clanking deck.

'OK. Panic over. They've obviously caught him. Get your engines started, we've not got all day.' It was one of the men who'd been sent down to search the cardeck, a flat Liverpool accent. Then an Irish voice said, 'They found the boy then? We didn't hear anything.'

The other man laughed. 'You wouldn't have. Little devil. He managed to get on shore apparently. They've got three of them anyway.'

There was another long pause. 'Can't see nothing, only policemen, and the army. What are they doing here? See enough of them as it is.' The Irish voice was muttering sourly, then there was a groaning wheeze as someone heaved himself up into Stan's truck.

Suddenly it moved off. In a cold sweat he waited for it to stop again, at some police barricade. He had a sour feeling in his stomach now and he wanted to be sick and empty his bowels, all at the same time.

But they weren't stopped. He felt the lorry lurch forward and swing round what must be a series of roundabouts before it seemed to settle down to a steadier speed with no stops or junctions, as if they were on a broad empty road. The driver had switched a radio on and was humming to it.

Stan wondered who the boy was that was supposed to be him, and why there were soldiers. He felt hungry again and he thought about his rucksack and the remains of Mary's money, lying with the fishes at the bottom of the sea. All the problems he'd put on that high dark shelf at the back of his mind had crept to the edge and started leering down at him.

He'd got nothing now. His rucksack had gone and his torch and the drugs packet. All he had left was the notebook, rolled up in the pocket of his trousers, one fifty-pence piece, and the Famous Five book, zipped in the front of his anorak. Useless.

Ratface had offered him big money. Why hadn't he taken it, when it would have bought freedom? It wasn't because Julius was a thief. He wasn't much better himself, now. Hadn't he been stealing and lying ever since he'd left London? It was because giving in to Julius Lodge would have been Giving In.

Huddled down in the muggy dark, jolted endlessly by the rattling lorry, Stan lost all sense of time. But it seemed only a few minutes before they were slowing down again. The truck felt as if it was swinging round in a huge circle now, then the engine stopped and he heard the driver get down.

This was it. He would surely come to the back and unload. Stan had to stop himself bursting out of the lorry and making a run for it, but he tried to straighten up slowly, pushing the tower of boxes apart so he could get out.

He heard footsteps crunching away from the cabin, then rich Irish voices in greeting.

'Is it Jimmy? At last, man. So what kept you this time?'

'Oh God, same old thing. Police all over the boat again.'

'Well, let's get this lot unloaded. The boss'll be in soon.'

'Aw stuff that, will you, for half an hour. I'm after having a bit of breakfast. At least give us a cup of tea.'

'All right, all right, but we'll have to make it quick.'

The voices faded and a door slammed to, then silence. Stan peeped out of the truck, then climbed down and looked around. He was in a big yard behind a row of houses, mean little terraces like the ones in Warrington. The windows were uncurtained and bleared with dirt, others were boarded up and at one end a house had been knocked down; he could see a black firegrate half-way up the wall. Two more lorries like his were parked across the yard in front of a newish brick building that looked like a small warehouse. The morning was dark and there was a light on inside.

He moved forward a step, his boots crunching on gravel and cinders. In the deserted yard the noise sounded like a small explosion; all was quiet apart from the faint hum of traffic from some unseen arterial road.

Voices floated across from the warehouse, then a door opened. Stan fled, down a rubble-filled entry knocking over cartons and a dustbin, right into another long terrace, left on to a broader street, unpeopled and dark under the steady drizzle.

People obviously still lived here. Some of the houses had been partly demolished, others stood empty, their doors and windows torn out, but here and there he noticed fresh curtains and new paint, a milk bottle not yet taken in. He retreated into the doorway of somebody's abandoned sitting-room, partly for cover, partly to get out of the rain, staring across the street at a long brick wall.

It was like a ghost city, no noise of shoppers or children, not even a dog. A few houses up a white net curtain twitched like an eyebrow and was still. In the silence Stan's nerves rested for a minute and then began to gather together again, planning their next move. He relaxed and leaned against the broken door-jamb, feeling a bit calmer.

Then a rumble started a few streets off and noise grew upon the terrace. Round the corner came an armoured car painted camouflage colours, with four soldiers, one at each corner, rifles up, in the firing position. The heavy machine crawled slowly along the street and Stan moved out of eyeshot, behind the doorway.

Three of the soldiers looked very young, one was hardly shaving, pink-faced and pimply, not much older than he was. As they passed out of sight he could see the wall again. The drizzle was lightening and the white-painted graffiti shone luminously, freshened up by the rain. 'Brits Out, Brits Out' Stan read, and in gigantic capitals 'PROVOS' and again 'Brits Go Home'. Underneath, more on its own, someone had written in childish print 'Our Terry Is Dead'.

Stan had known even before he'd climbed down into the yard, even before he'd heard them talking about the soldiers. It was when he'd listened to those two men talking, down in the cardeck. You didn't sail to Dublin by going up a lough. He remembered that lough from Geography, British Isles.

He'd got on the wrong boat in Liverpool. This wasn't Dublin at all, it was Belfast.

Northern Ireland. He felt numb all through. No prizes for working out how it had happened though. The Liverpool ferries didn't just go to Dublin, they went to the Isle of Man, too, and to Belfast; any fool knew that. Just because there was fighting over here it didn't mean nobody ever came near the place, people had to come sometimes, business people and men that worked for the government. They even tried to get you over for a holiday. That was a laugh. Come to sunny Belfast and get your head blown off.

Stupid, stupid, *stupid*. Getting to Dublin was a piece of cake, yet Stan Mellor had to go and get on the wrong boat because he'd not checked his details properly. 'Irish ferries' the sign had said, and that's what the paperboy had asked him, 'Going for the Irish ferry?' He could hear that flat Liverpool voice now. But there'd only ever been one Ireland for Stan. It was Dublin, and the wild green South where Sid was, on the Kellys' farm. It was his own fault, ending up in a hole like this; he was just plain thick.

For the second time since leaving London he felt like giving up. The hopeless weariness that had swept over him as he stood on Lime Street Station was on him again, but worse than before, his throat tightened and the tears pricked behind his eyes. It was useless carrying on with this, he'd never get across the border.

Even if he did get through and reach Joe Kelly's farm, what would he find? Vera was probably right, Sid could have moved on months ago or he might have met up with someone and got married, he liked girls. And old Joe might be dead too, like Mrs Kelly. The best people always died.

He didn't want to hang around any more, it was beginning to feel as if he'd spent half his life doing that; he

135

was going to start walking till he found a police station then he'd go in, and tell them who he was. By the end of the week he'd be right back where he started, except that it wouldn't be Auntie Marjorie looking after him but someone else, not nearly so kind. He'd be warm, fed and humiliated, and it'd serve him right.

He looked up at the heavy sky, rubbing at the tears and the rain on his cheeks till the skin was sore, then he laced old Jack's boots up very tight and stepped out into the street, moving off in the direction of the faint hum of traffic.

It was over.

Chapter Fourteen

He soon hit the main road again and began walking in the direction of the solid flow of cars and lorries. He wasn't planning to thumb any lifts though, he was fed up of funny questions and funny looks. Belfast couldn't be the best place for someone like him to attract attention anyway, people lived on their nerves over here.

Every week there were 'incidents' reported on the television news, shootings and bombings; they were ten a penny in this place. The violence seemed to come in spasms though, not much would happen for months then something really horrific would be all over the papers, like a pub with dozens of people in it getting blown apart, or someone having his legs torn off in a booby-trapped car. Stan didn't have a clue about why they were fighting. He only knew that Protestants made up one lot of terrorists and Catholics another, and that they both claimed to have right on their side.

Religion. It was no wonder people didn't believe in God any more. If the Martians landed 'Christians' would have a hard job explaining why they spent all their time blowing one another up. If it put off ordinary people like him there wouldn't be much hope of converting creatures from outer space, would there?

One of their teachers was Irish, Mr Mahoney, who took them for Chemistry. He'd talked to them once about the troubles in Ireland. Everything was buried deep in history, according to him. He didn't think the government had helped much in recent years though, bringing all the soldiers in. He'd looked really sad when he talked about it, Stan had remembered that. You always felt a bit embarrassed when teachers showed their feelings.

He didn't know what he thought about Northern Ireland himself, except that he wanted to get out of it quick.

It was a long hard slog into the centre of the city, but at least nobody stopped to ask him what he was doing, and he had no problem keeping his bearings because the main roads were good and very clearly signposted. As it became more built-up everything began to look cleaner and better cared for. The houses were new, box-like in their neat square gardens. It was all quite different from those low, beaten-up terraces near the docks, where he'd crawled out of the lorry.

When he saw the sign 'police station' pointing down a side-road, away from the traffic, he set off towards it doggedly, his head well down. Turning himself in was going to be the hardest thing yet. It meant he'd failed to carry out the most important plan of his life.

He didn't see the building properly till he'd drawn level with it, but when he looked up he recoiled. The place was so heavily protected it looked ready to withstand a siege, thick high walls decorated with pieces of broken glass and inside them, through double iron gates, huge coils of ferocious barbed-wire. Every window in the place was barred and the glass was that special black kind which only went one-way. It meant snipers couldn't take pot-shots at the people in the building because they were invisible. The police could look out though, and spot any funny business.

Stan retreated. If they made ordinary police stations into fortresses that resembled Colditz what must army barracks be like? It was the soldiers who got the real flak over here. He went slowly back to the main road and carried on walking. There'd been no sign of an entrance into that place though he'd not exactly hung about. Get-

138

ting in and finding someone to speak to was obviously quite an operation. It wasn't like their little sub-station near Auntie Marjorie's where old ladies wandered in asking about lost dogs, and cadging cups of tea from the bobby on duty.

As he walked on the grim grey fortress with its sightless black eyes towered up in his mind. The place had frightened him because it spelt out the country's unhappiness. Belfast kids could never have known anything else except bomb scares and shoot-outs, it must be ordinary life to them.

Children ought to grow up free from grown-up worries; Stan felt passionately about that because his own childhood had been one big mess. That was why, if he ever had kids of his own, he was going to make sure it was different for them.

After a very long walk he ended up in yet another shopping precinct, much larger than the one in Warrington and quite a bit bigger than Golden Cross Centre, near Auntie Marjorie's. It had all the same shops though, the same glossy tiles, the same fountains playing in the middle. It was as if every town centre in Britain had been cloned from some great master plan; this place could be anywhere. For a long time he just wandered about aimlessly, staring through a succession of plate-glass windows but not actually seeing anything. He couldn't think what to do next.

If there'd been a friendly London bobby doing his stint somewhere in the precinct, Stan might have got up enough courage to approach him and 'confess', but he couldn't see anyone like that. There were several RUC officers in dark green uniforms outside some of the shops but his heart failed him when he thought of approaching one of them. They all looked so grim and strained, not exactly friendly. Mind you, he couldn't blame them. Who'd want their job? They must live on their nerves.

They seemed to be patrolling the bigger stores because anyone who went in was stopped and questioned. Inside, no doubt, there would be a check-point where somebody frisked you to see if you were carrying weapons. He'd seen that kind of thing on the telly, in plays.

But Belfast wasn't a play and the worst thing about it was that all these military checks were merely routine, routine to all the ordinary-looking people going in and out of Littlewoods and Marks and Spencers, doing their ordinary shopping. He watched them covertly, listening in on their conversations. He liked the sing-song way they spoke, it was so different from the Lancashire voices. All flat they'd been, like flat caps.

He spent last fifty-pence in a snack bar on a mug of chocolate and a sticky bun, making it last a long time while he finished his Famous Five book. In Liverpool City Library he'd been rather secretive about what he was reading, in case people laughed, but he didn't bother here, he felt too tired and shocked. If only somebody in authority would come over and tackle him, then cart him off. Life would be taken out of his hands then and it'd be a relief.

But nobody took a blind bit of notice of him, not even the soldiers standing in twos and threes outside the big stores. He must surely look a sight by now too; Jack's baggy old flannels were filthy with oil and his anorak had a big tear in it from when he'd crawled under the lorry. He must be starting to smell too, he could smell himself.

What he wanted more than anything was to sleep, endlessly. He could quite understand why old ladies slept a lot, and tramps, and people with no jobs. Sleeping was escaping and when life didn't have much on offer, going unconscious for a bit was a good way of sliding out of it. The way things were looking now Stan felt like sliding out himself.

He couldn't just sit around though, doing absolutely nothing. This peculiar stupor he kept falling into, every time something went a bit wrong, was daft; he wasn't thinking straight. For example, he could have spent that fifty-pence on a phone call. The operator would have told him if Joe Kelly had a number and he could have tried dialling it.

But half of him didn't want to go that far, not now. Even if Sid hadn't moved on he'd still be hundreds of miles away, across the border. Stan didn't want a big issue made of the fact that he'd got himself from London to Ireland without anyone stopping him. His plan had been to walk into that farmhouse and stand there, right as ninepence, not go whingeing down a telephone that he was accidentally trapped and penniless, in grey Belfast.

He decided to walk again, back down that busy main road with the neat Lego houses all along it. Walking might clear his head. He could even go right back to the docks and see if there was a boat out that night. Not that he could get aboard legally, he'd have to sneak through somehow and that would probably prove impossible. The security this side would be like Fort Knox.

He put one sore foot in front of the other and pushed himself forwards mechanically, his head churning; whether to contact Sid anyhow and risk a big disappointment, or whether to find someone in authority and tell them who he was; whether to go south and try and get himself across the border or whether to sneak on a boat and go back to Liverpool. His brain plunged about hopelessly, grasping at the whirl of possibilities, deciding nothing. Everything had fallen in on him and he wanted out.

Tonight he was going to sleep for a very long time and he wasn't planning beyond that.

Eventually he hit Edith Street again, the little old terrace that had taken him from the bomb-site area on to the arterial road. He was still a good way from the docks, according to the signs, though he could see huge cranes on the skyline. Yet when he saw the street he turned down it. The sky was darkening already and the afternoon wearing away. This place, he remembered, was a maze of half-demolished houses, it just might provide him with somewhere to sleep for the night. A good long kip would put off the decision about what to do next until morning and he might feel a bit tougher then, a bit less inclined to give up.

He poked about in the debris of the waste land for some considerable time, weighing up possibilities with a queer feeling of childish excitement. With no money, no food, and no water to wash in, life had become extremely simple. Perhaps that was why drop-outs were into poetry and stuff; they didn't sit worrying about mortgages and where to buy fresh chickens and redecorating their front rooms. When you didn't own anything life was reduced to bare essentials and the mind went free.

At last he found an old mattress on a rubbish heap, dragged it off and pulled it into the doorway of an empty house; then he saw a pillow in the same place, mouldy-green but reasonably dry, and he took that too. The ceiling of the doorless shell looked sound enough and there was a staircase, still intact, going up out of one corner. He could sleep up there, it might be drier. On the other hand he'd be better off down here if anybody spotted him and started making trouble. He could get away more easily. Anyhow, he wasn't ready to bed down yet. The night was young and he needed supplies.

Two houses at the far end of Edith Street definitely looked lived in. There must be people round here anyway, even if they did keep behind closed doors. Why else would the soldiers come round on patrol? On the step of number 16, a smart little establishment with net curtains and a newly painted front door, there were three pints of milk and a sliced loaf in a plastic bag. Stan stared down at them. There'd been one milk bottle here this morning, but now they'd bred. And where had the loaf come from? And why?

He wasn't all that hungry at the moment but he'd got to think ahead. Nobody was going to collect this lot now, the people at number 16 must have got stuck somewhere. You didn't leave milk out all day on purpose. He grabbed one of the bottles, shoved the loaf down the big pocket on the front of his anorak, and pelted back along the pavement to his mattress in the deserted house. Just in case.

It was raining again, the sort of rain that sets in with a vengeance and falls all night. Stan leaned against the door-jamb and stared out at the littered desolation of the abandoned street, swigging from his milk bottle and chewing on a slice of damp white pap. The bread tasted of nothing but it was food, filling up his stomach and comforting him. Then, as he watched the rain thickening, and blowing in waves along the terrace, something far away exploded with an almighty bang and the echo of a single massive thump shook the walls all round him. At the same moment somebody coughed somewhere, over his head.

His eyes crept over to the staircase in the corner. All the treads were littered with rubble but the crude banister rail gleamed dully. He edged over to it silently, but the small crunch of his boots over the ravaged ground spat like shrapnel.

At the foot of the stairs he stopped and listened again. Far off, in the invisible city, he could hear the shrill of a fire-engine. He climbed slowly, kicking away the rubble. At the top was a closed door, lime-green with blistered paint. Stan edged it open with the toe of his boot.

Then everything happened too quickly. The door gave way and he was pulled forwards into a warm fug. A cold hand hooked itself around his neck and someone was kneeing him in the stomach, pushing him back till he crumpled up against a wall. Stan shut his eyes and flung his arms up instinctively, trying to protect his face.

Chapter Fifteen

Somebody said, 'Open your eyes, and put your hands right up. *Not Like That*. Over your head. Put them together.' The Somebody was pulling at his fingers, twisting them right back. Then something cracked. Stan screamed and the Somebody slapped him hard across the face.

'*Shut it*. Someone'll hear you. Now open your eyes or I'll hit you again.'

He opened them. The person who'd done the kicking had his face thrust right up to him and he was feeling Stan all over, frisking him like the soldiers did in the shops, digging into his pockets. All he found was the bread. Stan thought he was going to start kicking him again but he took a step back and stared hard.

It was a boy, about Stan's height but much thinner and very pale. They could be about the same age, give or take a few months, it was hard to tell. He had reddish hair, very long, and matted with knots. Stan could smell it. The whole place stank of human beings, of hair and sweat and urine. There was a food smell too, and the whiff of paraffin mixed in with it. The warmth was coming from a small heater that puttered away in a corner on the filthy floor.

Slowly Stan looked back into the boy's eyes. They were little and brown, the only cold brown eyes he'd ever seen. The mouth was a short, lipless line, the nose hooked and biggish, with a white scar jagged across it. He wore jeans and a green sweater with cloth patches.

'What d'you think?' he said to someone behind him, turning round. 'No, stay there. Keep the gun on him. I said, *What do you think*?' The question was barked out, now.

'I'm sure ah don't know, Jerry. What *d'you* think, Jerry?'

This voice was young and frightened, not much more than a whimper. Standing in front of an old blanket that had been nailed in many thicknesses over a window was a tiny boy with a grown-up face. It was as if his head had kept on growing long after his body had given up, taking on the lines and creases of age, but still attached to a child's frame. His skin was greenish pale and the thin hair looked greenish too. Under the small eyes and snub of a nose was a huge mouth, all out of proportion. His enormous ears stuck straight out like a goblin's.

He was holding a pistol at arm's length, as if he thought it might go off in his hand without warning. Stan's eyes crept down to it in disbelief; it had got to be a toy. It trembled as the boy trembled.

'Oh Jesus, put the gun down. You're useless.'

'OK, Jerry. Sorry, Jerry,' the other one whispered and slumped down on to a broken stool, still shaking. Stan thought of Elspeth and that same greenish terror. He was filled with pity for the frightened, ugly boy. He wanted to smash the other one up, and put his arms around him.

Suddenly the one in charge hooked his foot round Stan's ankle and he fell heavily, something sharp sticking into him as he went down. He was back on his feet again, knotting his fists for a fight, when Jerry said, 'OK, OK. Relax, can't you. I'm not going to do anything to you. Yet.'

He gave a funny, twisted smile as Stan snatched a

146

quick look at him, chilled by the small hard eyes and the little mouth, the grey emptiness of the face.

'Where you from?'

Stan didn't answer.

'C'mon. What you doing here? *I'm asking you a question*,' and he delivered a neat sideways kick into Stan's thigh.

'I came over from Liverpool,' he stammered. 'I hid. On the boat.'

The thin boy closed in on him, interested, almost impressed. In the warm gloom the little goblin boy crept up to listen too.

'And you got away with it. You got on shore?'

'Yes. I hid in a truck, on the cardeck.'

'What you doing here, then, in Belfast?'

'It was a mistake. I'm . . . I was trying to get to Dublin, to find my brother.'

'*Jesus, Mary and Joseph!*' Bully Boy actually laughed.

'You English then?' Goblin Child whispered.

The other one swung round and pushed at him, thrusting his flat pasty face back with the palm of his hand.

'Shut your face, you. What d'you bloody think he is? Chinese? You're supposed to be on the look-out anyhow. Get on with it, or I'll thump you.'

Goblin scuttled off and turned back to his spyhole in the blanketed window. Then there was silence. Bully pulled his mouth about weirdly and narrowed his eyes cowboy-fashion, still staring.

Suddenly Stan got to his feet. 'If you've finished kicking me,' he said, 'I'd like to stand up, that is, if you don't object. My leg's gone to sleep. Who do you think you are anyway, John Wayne?'

Bully opened his mouth, the pale hard face looked just a bit stupid now, at a loss for what to say next. In the thick silence the dwarf at the window sniffed quietly, rubbing at his eyes with a filthy sleeve.

'I'm going,' Stan said. 'I've got to find a post office.

Where – ' but as he pushed forward something roared into the street and stopped outside the house. A car door banged and somebody below knocked sharply three times at the bottom of the rickety staircase.

In seconds the boy called Jerry was on the other side of the blistered green door, talking to someone from half-way down the steps. Stan listened hard but could make no sense of it. It was all codes and numbers, and the names of streets. Then he heard, '*Now*? No, can't do it. Something's come up.' A pause, then whispering, too mumbled for him to hear properly.

Suddenly the voice hardened and he said loudly, 'OK. *OK*. I'll be over. You got everything?' A pause, then, 'Yes, you'd *better* be, *bloody* sure.'

The car roared off again and Jerry was back in the room before Goblin had got back to his position by the window. Stan stopped, half-way to the stairs.

'Now, *look you*,' and Jerry grabbed Goblin by the shoulders, kneading bony knuckles into his shoulder blades, 'I'm going to see Beatty. Get over there and *don't move*. I'll be straight back. Here's the gun. If he tries anything, use it.'

At the door he stopped and looked back into the room with Stan and Goblin Child still staring across at him. He took a small pistol from his jacket and rubbed at it lovingly, in a kind of caress. Then he disappeared.

'Put the gun down, will you?' Stan said when he was sure they were on their own. 'It might go off. I'm getting out of here.'

But Goblin Child jerked forward, filling the stairway.

'Don't go yet, don't go for about ten minutes, then it'll be OK. He's goin' across the city, y'see.' Now Jerry was gone his whole body sagged. He hardly seemed to notice when Stan carefully unwrapped his fingers from round the gun and placed it over their heads on a rickety shelf, behind some tins.

'What's your name?'

'Liam Boyle. What's yours?'

'Stan.'

'Did you really hide on that boat, or was it lies?' His flat pale eyes grew big as he looked at Stan.

'It's true.'

'What about your mam? Does your mam know?'

Stan shook his head.

'Well, my mam'll kill me, if she ever finds out about this. Three weeks we've bin here, waitin', and I'm bloody sick of it, I can tell you.'

'Doesn't she know where you are?'

He shook his head. 'We all went one night, when we got Jerry's message like.'

'Jerry – *that* one?' Stan jerked his head backwards, at the stairway.

'Jerry Hogan, he's in charge like.'

Stan said, 'But why don't you just go home? You're frightened of him, aren't you? Why stay here with him? He's a thug. Look how he treats you. He's a coward too, going off and leaving you here.' Weariness and lack of proper food was loosening his tongue like drink. Fear was beginning to turn his mind inside-out. He could hear himself rambling on and on wildly, unable to stop, and he was sure the boy was listening, that he was winning him round. 'Look how he kicked me,' he went on, 'he's a sadist and he's a coward too – '

But suddenly the flat goblin features blanked and the boy came away from the window, shouting shrilly, 'He's no *coward*. Jerry Hogan's *no coward*. *You*, shut your gob. You don't know what you're talking about. He's fightin' for a free Ireland. His dad and his brother, they were both killed in the fightin', his mam's goin' off her head an' all and won't go out of the house no more – oh it's terrible for him.'

'Why don't you just go home?' Stan repeated, talking slurred, like a man doped and drunk. 'What are you all playing at? Why don't your parents send the police out after you?'

'It's what I'm telling you, man,' the tiny, shrunken boy said in his piercing, little girl's voice. 'There's a war on, nobody's *playin'*. D'you know where you are? This isn't fairyland.' His voice was bitter now. He sounded like Victor, or Julius Lodge. 'D'you know where *this* is?' he repeated.

'Course I do. I'm not thick. It's Belfast.'

Silence unrolled between them. It was just a word to Stan, a word with a string of others. Always the same, and the same pictures on the telly, ambulances, and fires in streets, the Falls Road, the Crumlin Road and the Shankhill Road. Prods and Provos. Petrol bombs. The Maze prison. He didn't understand any of it. It was supposed to be about religion too. But how could it be?

'You a Prod then?'

Liam Boyle was staring at him curiously and a pale gleam of interest had crept into the flat, fish-like eyes.

'I'm nothing . . . *nothing* . . .' Stan said. 'I don't believe in God.' But unease was plucking at him. 'I'm – we're – I sometimes go to St Oswald's church, in Green Street, with Auntie Marjorie. It's Church of England.'

'So you're a Protestant.'

'No, I'm nothing. She makes me go, I've *told* you!'

'Dunt matter. That's what you are.'

The two boys got up and went for the stairs at the same moment, but Stan was a head taller and twice as broad.

'Let me get out, Liam. I'm only trying to find my brother. I didn't know there was anyone here, honest to God. I don't want to get mixed up with your gang, or whatever it is.'

But Liam was standing between him and the stairs.

'I can't. They'll get me. They'll put Jack Beatty on to me, and he's wild. That's what the men do when their people step out of line, they shoot their own. We're not a gang anyway. This is a proper division. It's official and Jerry's in charge. He's not frightened of anyone neither. He's shot someone already. You can't go. If you go they'll kill me.' He was lying across the stairs now, all humped up, trying to fill the space with his thin, sweating body, and he was crying.

Stan looked down. He could have kicked him out of the way quite easily, but the pinched old man's face was a mixture of pleading bewilderment and sheer terror. Goblin Child clutched at Stan's boots now, and sobbed.

The boy couldn't leave him. He turned hopelessly back into the airless hide-out, wondering if there was time to get the gun and hide it properly. Three weeks they'd been waiting. What for? Stan felt afraid for his own life.

'It's all right,' he said to Liam. 'It's all *right*,' and he patted him. The sound of crying took him right back to the old days, before Mrs Kelly, in the homes. He just couldn't bear it.

Then, down below, there were sounds of Jerry Hogan coming back with the others.

Chapter Sixteen

Altogether there were five of them, Jerry Hogan, Liam Boyle, Jack Beatty and two more, twin brothers called Peter and Pat McDowell. Beatty was the worst. He was enormous. Greasy black hair hanging down in strings, coarse tanned face, brown teeth. He puffed and grunted at the others all the time, and smoked endless cigarettes. His gun was a big one, black and old-fashioned looking, more like a cowboy's six-shooter. He sat on the floor twirling it round one finger and laughing at Stan.

'Jesus, Mary and Joseph, a tame Prod. And our Jerry tells me you stowed away on the boat?'

Stan didn't answer.

'It's not true, is it?'

He just nodded.

'C'mon. It's you I'm talking to. Not true, is it?'

'Yes, it's true,' Stan said, through his teeth. 'I thought it was going to Dublin.' It sounded so stupid, so innocent, in this world of guns and blood, where boys were armed and looked like wizened old men.

The two brothers were standing at a table carefully filling empty salmon tins with old nails and powder. They looked pleasant enough, gingery and fresh-faced; they might have been boys in his class.

'Don't tell bloody lies.'

'It was in the newspapers,' Stan said. 'Have a look, if you don't believe me. You'll probably find something in that lot,' and he jerked his head at a heap of papers in a

152

corner. Jack Beatty went on smoking, and grinning at him, but Jerry was already at the pile, squatting over it and smoothing out the paper on top, studying it closely.

They all had cigarettes. The air grew rapidly foul and thick and soon he could only half see them through the fug. He was in the window corner with Liam standing over him miserably, holding the pistol that had been rescued from its shelf.

'Well, you've come at a good moment, sonny boy,' Jack Beatty sneered. 'This thing's big, so big we've not really got enough manpower. *See? So get over there*, will ya!' He leaned forward, plucking Stan off the floor, then half pushed, half threw him across to the blanketed window.

Then the three of them moved at once. They must have planned it beforehand, around Stan. He'd never been so important. The ginger brothers were over to him in seconds, and they took an arm each. Beatty tied his feet together with thick cord and secured the free end to a rusty hook in the floor. The cord went round his waist, then round and up again, tied cuttingly, spiralling to his shoulder. The McDowell brothers pulled, tested, knotted, and tugged, with Beatty standing over them, grunting advice. When they'd finished Stan was all trussed up like a turkey at Christmas except for one thing, his right hand and arm were free.

Something was pushed at him by one of the brothers and Beatty hissed, 'It's loaded. And the ammunition's live. You've got your own look-out. *Here.*' Stan's face was pushed up against the damp blanket and he found himself peering through a jagged slit down into the street.

'It's true what he says, Jack.' Jerry Hogan was holding up a copy of the *Belfast Telegraph*. Stan could see three photographs, though the headlines were blurred. 'Never,' Jack Beatty said scornfully, sucking on his cigarette. '*Him?* Don't give me that.'

'Read it yourself then, if you can read,' Hogan said contemptuously. 'And clear off out. I want to talk to him.'

The two boys stared at one another, Stan's blunt, handsome features all but lost in dirt and a shag of hair, suspicious, still not trusting. Jerry Hogan's face, smaller, ungenerous, was now set in a hard questioning gaze, but there was an intensity about it, almost wonder. 'How did you do it?' he whispered.

'How did I do what?'

'The whole bit – after you quit, in London? Didn't you know he was after you, this Julius?'

'Not at first. Didn't know I was carrying anything, did I . . . but then, when he kept showing up . . . well, I got a bit suspicious, didn't I?'

'Says here he tried to shoot you. That true, is it?' Stan shook his head. 'Dunno really, I reckon he was just trying to frighten me. He did have a gun, in Warrington, he fired across some waste ground where I was hiding.'

'What kind of gun was it?' Jerry was clutching at his sleeve. 'Was it like this one?' and he thrust his own under Stan's nose.

'I . . . I don't know. I didn't see it. I'm not interested in guns.'

The cold irony smell of the metal was beginning to turn his stomach. He turned his face away, and looked through the slit in the blanket.

They'd chosen their position with care. The empty house overlooked a street lamp, the only one intact for miles around. All the others had been smashed up by gangs, or by the army, for extra cover. This lamp was still working, spreading a blurred circle of light over the wet pavement, illuminating the mean terraces for several yards on either side. There was nobody about. A cat crept out from under a fence and stretched itself, its bottom high and tight, its tail a question mark.

He could still feel Jerry Hogan behind him, and he

turned round very slowly. The boy had picked up the newspaper again and he was poring over it, looking from Stan's face to the row of photographs, going through the newsprint slowly with his finger, like a child that can only just read.

He admired anyone with guts and he was fascinated by Stan. It was true that he was a Brit and so part of the war machine they were all fighting. British soldiers had gunned down his father and his brother, Pat, and it was all one. And yet . . . look what he'd done. Got himself from London to Belfast by hiding in lorries and stowing away on a boat, while the police were spreading a net for him because of these men that were working a drugs racket. This news story said that Julius Lodge had been inside once for robbery with violence and that the other had been done for fraud.

'Where's your mam and dad?' he asked suddenly. 'Why didn't you try 'n' get to them?'

Stan didn't answer. He stared at the floor, moving an empty fag packet about with his foot.

'C'mon. I've asked you a question.' The voice was hard again, but Jerry didn't touch him. He didn't want to hurt him any more, not this one. But he had to know.

'I don't live with my mum. I've always been . . . in care.' When it came to it Stan could hardly say the last bit. His whole life was in those two words.

'In care? What's that then?'

'Don't you know?'

Hogan shook his head.

'It's when the welfare people find somewhere for you to go, when your parents . . . can't look after you.'

And he felt tears behind his eyes, impossible tears running together in his throat.

Hogan was looking at him in silence and with brimming eyes Stan looked back steadily. He could see no mean suspicion now in the small, narrow face, no threat, no hate. For a minute something had cleared in it. Hogan was thinking, and trying not to think, of his own mother at home, wondering where on earth he was, half-mad with the terror of everything as the city exploded around her, thinking of his dad and their Pat, wondering if he'd been shot too.

'I should go back and see to our mam,' he said, but to himself, not Stan. 'But we've got this job first. I'll go after.'

On the way over in Laffetty's van he'd argued with Jack Beatty over the English boy. Beatty was all for getting rid of him. 'He's fell into our laps, so let's just get rid of him. It's what they'd expect us to do,' he'd said.

But Hogan was less certain. The Organization had definite procedures about everything, what to do about the army, what to do about stray Prod kids on your patch, what to do with anyone seen fraternizing with the enemy. But they'd not said what to do about a Brit, a boy of your own age, who'd accidentally got himself into the middle of a big operation, like the one he and Jack Beatty were on with now. A thing like that just couldn't happen. But it had.

He'd said, 'We can't just shoot him, Jack, he's not done nothing. They wouldn't want us to shoot him. If it ever got out it'd look bad for us. We must keep hold of him, and see what Michael says.'

'What if the place goes up?' Beatty had said thickly. He actually wanted to kill Stan, it was something he'd quite enjoy. Anyhow, he didn't like anyone cleverer than he was.

Hogan grunted back, 'He'll just have to go with us, that's all. Michael makes the decisions, not us.'

Stan was fingering the gun they'd given him. 'What am I supposed to do with this?'

'Oh, don't you know?' Beatty's sarcasm was honey-sweet. 'Young Boyle here'll tell you,' and he gave Goblin Child a poke with his own weapon. 'Go on, you tell him, Liam.'

'Yes Jack, sure Jack. We – we're on duty here, see? If anyone comes on to the street we signal. Isn't that so, Jack? You tell him, Jack.' His voice trembled desperately.

'You're snipin', man,' Beatty cut in heavily. 'You don' signal, you *fire*. Anything comin' round that corner gets it. OK?'

'I see. Postman, milk, anything,' Stan said, too loudly. Sheer disbelief had made him desperate. Jack was on to him before he could draw breath, winding him with huge knuckles, making him groan.

'There'll be a patrol before dark, see? And there'll be others. We bin waitin' for ever. If it don't happen we make it happen, get it? It's all laid on, right across the city. You shoot them or we'll shoot you. They're all Brits, and you're one too. Neat innit?'

The gang settled down and talked to each other in mumbled whispers. Stan's back was to the room but his ears strained painfully to catch what they were saying, he felt as if blood would come pouring out of his eardrums, he was listening so hard. Liam was next to him glued to his own spyhole. They exchanged looks once and the tiny boy smiled nervously at him and pointed to the vest pocket of his shirt. Under the grease marks he could just make out the shadow of a knife.

Twice somebody sneaked up to the house, knocked out a signal and got Hogan downstairs to talk to them. He always came back with papers. Stan thought there must be another hide-out, like theirs, in a street nearby, and that somebody would bring the signal from there.

He heard Jerry whispering to Beatty, 'Look at this, will you? It's from Michael.'

'He says to leave him here.'

Their voices were very low. The McDowells were over by the stairs lifting a thick cable from a box, Liam was huddled by the blanket, not paying much attention. But Stan heard.

Everyone had a gun and Stan had seen two rifles in a

corner. The table was covered with old tins and heaps of metal scraps; there were some tape-cassette boxes too, filled with bits of metal and powder, then sellotaped together in twos and threes.

They were ordered to leave him in the house if they had to use 'the lorry', which he figured must be on standby somewhere, if things went wrong. If there was an explosion, and that's the way it was looking, the house would go up. And he'd be in it.

He looked hard at Hogan, his lips framing a question, but the other boy wouldn't look. He'd sagged down on top of the pile of newspapers and was staring at the floor.

Beatty said jubilantly, 'Told ya, told ya, didn't I? You was bloody mad to think – '

'Shut your great mouth, you, I don't want to *hear* it,' and Hogan put his hands over his ears, to shut out the fat roar of Jack Beatty's laughter.

Stan wondered what the grand plan was but could only get fragments. When the 'signal' came Jerry's division was obviously going to cover from the windows. Two would be positioned downstairs with explosive devices. But it would all start with a fire somewhere else, and random shooting in empty houses. This way they would lure the soldiers down this street and into an ambush of bullets.

He stared down outside and saw a lorry trundle slowly past with a clanking exhaust. He stiffened. Jerry was already at the blanket but Liam said, 'It's all right, it's only Laffetty,' and Hogan went straight back to his papers.

Behind Stan someone was scraping back a heavy piece of furniture and he could feel cold air. He tried to turn round but immediately got a sharp thump between the shoulders, and a voice said, 'Mind your face, you.' It was Beatty.

Please, Stan said silently. Please let something happen

158

to end this, before people get killed. Please help us. It's all mad.

Belfast jargon. You heard it all the time. You slid so easily from the evening news into the detective thrillers and all the guns and murder seemed make-believe then. Those letters the newsmen reeled off, RUC and UDR, UFF and IRA. His mind had absorbed everything and understood nothing. Would it have been any different if this gang had been Protestant and not Catholic? They'd still have put a gun in his hand. They'd still have made him fight.

Everybody looked so young. Nobody there could be more than seventeen and the other boy-gangs across the city were probably children too. They didn't play English against Germans in the Belfast streets. They played a dead Catholic for a dead Prod. It had always been like that, according to Mr Mahoney. It was history.

One of the McDowells was sent over to loosen the cord on the iron ring, and in doing so he turned Stan round roughly. Now he could see where the cold air was coming from. They'd pushed back an old dresser and in the wall behind was a gaping hole where a couple of dozen bricks had been hacked out. Beyond was soft, damp-smelling darkness. The whole gang had gathered round it.

Jerry Hogan spoke quietly, through clenched teeth, 'If I say, and *only if I say*, we all go through. Show me your lights.' Each boy fished in jacket and trousers. Four flat red plastic torches were laid in a row on the table. Jerry tested them all in turn. 'OK. You can put them away.'

'What about Laffetty?' Peter McDowell said nervously. 'Are you sure he'll be there, if we need him?'

Jerry reddened with temper. 'Am I sure he'll be there? Huh.' He mimicked the boy's thin, rather reedy voice, then spat on the floor. 'He's there already. The lorry's in position. Let's hope we don't need it.'

'What about me?' Stan said, though he knew.

There was a thick silence and the gang all stared at Hogan.

'We're leaving you here. That's my orders.'

Nobody moved and the silence loomed over them, like darkness. As he turned away he muttered through his teeth, 'Sorry,' but so low that only Stan could hear.

Liam was looking at the tins and cassette-boxes on the table.

'Jerry,' he got out in a high voice, tight with nerves. 'If you don't mind me sayin' it, Jerry, you're too near the table with yer fag.'

'Shut it, you,' Hogan spat at him. But he doused the cigarette butt all the same, in an empty milk bottle.

So Laffetty was ready with the lorry. Everyone put his cigarette out and checked his gun, and the atmosphere grew heavy. It had got to be soon, Stan knew that much.

Chapter Seventeen

Hours seemed to pass, and the little street was grave-quiet, the nearest thing to life was the faint light of the city flickering over the roofs. Gradually, behind him, Stan could make out the heavy breathing of sleep. In the silence somebody, he thought Beatty, started to snore gently.

He felt so awake he believed he would never sleep again. His eyes kept watering, screwed up to observe the little street-scene cameoed through the ripped blanket. The cold gun, just under his nose, had a pungent smell. They had tied his feet and arm so tightly that his flesh was beginning to lose all feeling. So when Liam crouched down in the darkness and began to saw through the cords with his penknife, Stan's body hardly responded. He felt it only as a slight loss of tension, like a coiled spring made limp through overpulling.

Liam was mouthing at him, so low it was almost soundless, but Stan read his lips. 'They'll try to blow this place up, if they can. They've made things. They want to destroy what they leave behind them. You must get out. Don't come with us. Don't jump into the street. The army have orders to shoot on sight. If you can get through the –'

But he never finished because a car suddenly roared round the corner and stopped outside the house. There was a rapid, repeated dinning sound down below, on something metal, with no attempt to dull it. It went on and on and on, till they were all awake, and standing up.

The signal.

Pat McDowell shook Beatty into life and he came to, foully, with spit dripping from his mouth. He got up, slavering and swearing.

Hogan made for the window, breathing quickly, shouldering Stan aside to get at the slit with his own weapon. He took Stan's gun away and pushed it into his belt, his body rigid. Now the crunch had come he couldn't let anyone else do his killing, and he would do whatever the Organization expected, even though, as Stan had detected, he'd softened a bit towards him. The boy prayed he would not look down, that the darkness would hide the cut cords round his feet.

He turned into the room and stared about dumbly, but nobody took any notice of him now. The house was suddenly rocked by a series of dull thumps and there was a crackle of gunfire, then an explosion, this time nearer. 'Dead on time,' he heard Hogan mutter to himself, looking at a watch.

The door on to the stairs had been opened and Beatty stood at the top, his gun pointing at the floor. The McDowells had already clattered down out of sight with the debris from the table. One was desperately trying to untangle some kind of cable from a spool.

'For God's sake, hurry up, you fool,' Beatty whispered. Tension had made him quiet, and somehow smaller.

Faintly, through the blanket, came the wail of fire-engines. Jerry took a step back and looked across at Beatty, his thin face disconcerted, touched with fear. He was opening his mouth but the words were drowned by gunfire. It was very near, the repeated small explosions seemed to be coming from all sides. Stan's ears sang with pain and a shot ripped the blanket and started a slow smoulder, bedding into the wall. Liam dropped down beside him.

He whispered, 'There's a tank, Jerry . . . there's two tanks.' He bobbed up again to the blanket, 'I can – oh *God* . . .' His voice dried up. Hogan pushed him out of the way and looked for himself.

Nobody in the room had fired a single shot but the noise was huge now. It was as if they were sealed up inside metal walls while bullets spanged down on them, underneath and over their heads, cracking and exploding inside their very brains. Stan wanted to scream.

'We should get out, Hogan,' Beatty yelled loudly, in panic, forgetting the silence of conspiracy now fear was on him. 'We should get out *now*.' The plan, whatever it had been, was going wrong. Nobody was in his place or trying to do anything quietly. The McDowells had come back up the stairs at a run and the door was slammed and bolted.

'Jerry, Jerry,' one of them panted, 'the police are out there. I don't know what's gone wrong but the place is crawling. Someone's been shot on Walton Street.'

'Have you got the cable?'

The brothers nodded together, Tweedledum and Tweedledee. But these were not Humpty Dumpty faces, split stupidly with inane grins. Their faces were bloodless, drawn tight with uncertainty, centuries old in that moment.

Beatty bent down and pulled something out from underneath the door. A whitish cord, a kind of soft rope, snaked out. He laid it across the floor as far as the hole.

'You soaked it good?'

'We used all of it.'

Jerry stood by the hole and signalled.

'*OK*,' and he pointed into the darkness. They were all fumbling for their torches now with sweaty fingers. There was a lull in the gunfire but at the back of the terrace came a sound of breaking glass and something thudding against the brickwork. The hole was low and they crawled through singly, first Beatty then the McDowells, clambering over heaps of rubble, their small torchbeams finding the hole in the wall of the next house, and the next, until, six houses down, they would reach a yard where Laffetty was waiting with his lorry.

But nerves had made them sluggish and false-footed.

'C'mon, *c'mon,*' snapped Hogan, 'they'll be through in a minute.' His back was to the room and he was shining a bigger flashlight into the next house, picking out their way, to hurry them up. Stan tried to step forward away from the wall and fell over. He was still tethered to the rusty hook by a single cord. He bent down to pull at it but Liam was already there with his penknife, sawing.

Then Hogan turned round and looked. He saw the knife and the frayed ropes. Stan free. The small boy stood up and his child's voice was piercing and shrill. 'Jerry, we can't leave him, Jerry. Please. You can't do it to him. I was only –' He stopped. Hogan's face was chalk-white, the blood washing away from it in a single wave. He looked from Stan, crouched down at his feet, to Liam with the penknife, then back to Stan. Time stopped. Then Liam began to weep, a wild pain-filled howling that cut into Stan's heart with its old, raw memories. Jerkily, Hogan grabbed at him and pushed him forward into the hole.

'*You*, go after the others. When you get to the yard you'll have to jump. There's a trapdoor in the roof of Laffetty's lorry. Mind how you do it, or you'll break your legs. The code name's Emerald. Use it or they'll shoot you.'

Stan turned back towards the rough square of light. Liam was cowering in the corner by the rifles, and somebody was pushing at the door. The hinges were already giving way.

'Do as I'm telling you. You don't know when your luck's in. If you don't I'll use this,' and he waved his gun.

Stan fell forward into the hole, stumbling towards the far wavering torches. In the small boarded-up bedrooms the firing and noise outside was dulled to a soft rumble.

As he crawled blindly forward, he heard matches rattling, then one, two being struck. Then a fizzing noise as the cable took hold, and a smell of petrol.

'Ah, *don't, Jerry*.' He was nearly at the last house but the voice was so clear, the boy could have been inches from his side. There were two quick shots, screaming, then silence, and he saw Hogan's wide torchbeam dipping and lurching out of the dark.

He shouted 'Emerald!' and hands reached up, pulling him down through the trapdoor in the lorry roof. Seconds later Jerry Hogan came through. Somebody banged on the cabin wall and Laffetty moved off.

Only when they were in the lorry, rattling out of the yard, did they hear the explosion, and the rattle of falling glass and timbers as the house fell in.

Chapter Eighteen

'Peter! Get over here, will you.'

Hogan's voice was high and strangled, he'd slumped down in a corner on a heap of sacking, jamming Stan up against the front wall. His heart was thumping so violently the boy could actually feel it.

One of the McDowells went over to the back of the truck and squatted down by the slit in the tarpaulins. He positioned his gun and crouched over it, breathing fast.

'D'you think they'll be after us, Jerry? What are you expecting?'

'How the bloody hell do I know? Stick to what you're doing, and belt up.'

The lorry space was dimly lit by Hogan's big torch. He'd pulled out the carrying ring and fastened it with string to a nail in the roof. The white circle of light bobbed and danced crazily as the lorry picked up speed. Soon the city glare through the slit faded and turned black.

There were four of them, Hogan and the twins, and Stan. Beatty must be up with Laffetty in the driving cabin. The atmosphere was thick. Pat McDowell pulled out a cigarette and tried to light it, but his hand wobbled.

'Put the bugger out,' Hogan snarled from his corner. 'We're carrying petrol. Are you blind?' He was examining his gun carefully.

'Where's Liam?' Pat wasn't afraid of Hogan and his voice was sharp. Stan, hunched up against him, couldn't see Jerry's face but he felt eyes on him, travelling down slowly over his matted curls, his greasy forehead, his dry lips.

'Dead.'

'*Dead?*'

There was silence, then Pat said, 'Jerry – *Jerry*! You didn't leave him when the bomb went off? Surely you didn't leave him? In Christ's *name* . . .'

'Shut it. Just *shut it*. I've had all I can stand, from you and everyone else.' Hogan was on his feet and Stan heard his knuckles crunch up against the other boy's teeth. 'Shut it, or I'll dump you.'

'But why, Jerry?'

'Because he betrayed us.'

'*Betrayed? Him?* What d'he do? What you talkin' about?'

'*Him*, Boyle, that one. He undid the Prod. He was tellin' him how to get away if there was a shoot-out. They were working it out together. I saw them.'

'But, *Jerry* –'

'So I shot him. Orders. The Organization can't carry people like him. Anyway, he was pathetic.'

Stan whispered from his corner, 'It's me you should've shot, I'd have thought it was a gift. You said they'd told you to leave me behind, whoever it is that gives you your orders.'

It was too dark for him to see Hogan's face now, but when it came the voice sounded curiously broken, all choked with a hard emotion. He spoke very quietly. 'You're nothing, you. It was an emergency, and *in* an emergency the officer in charge decides. Michael was wrong, you're nothin'. You're not part of the British Government War Machine.' He spelled out the words painfully, as if he was reading them with great difficulty, from an official manual. 'You . . . you're just a bloody fool. You should have stayed at home in bloody London, you should.'

His voice broke completely and the fragments of

speech were swallowed up in the jolting darkness. The truth was different. He couldn't have left Stan to be blown to pieces. In a different world they'd have been mates. Deep inside he knew that Stan was all right, he'd got guts that one, more guts than this lot put together. Beatty was just a clod who enjoyed beating people up, he understood nothing really. The McDowell twins were close and tight-lipped, always sticking together, thick as thieves. As for Liam Boyle, he'd always been the weakest link in the chain. Jerry had warned Michael about him. Wet his pants sooner than pull a gun. He didn't regret Liam Boyle.

Rhythmical tapping was coming through from the driving cabin, a series of beats grouped carefully together. After a minute Hogan tapped back. Then he sat down on some sacks in a corner and pulled out some chewing-gum.

'OK so far, Peter. We'll be through in about ten minutes. Anything doing at the back?'

'All clear, Jerry.'

'Will there be soldiers?' Stan said numbly. He meant, Will there be guns? The spattering of bullets before some final massive explosion? A scream was unwinding itself somewhere deep in his belly, travelling up through him, slowly, and he was beginning to shake. He kept seeing Liam's flat pasty face, remembering his terror. He saw the police car stopping outside the house in a Belfast terrace, somebody climbing out of it and going in to tell his mam.

'Oh yeah,' Hogan said spitefully, 'we'll come into the Republic at a major check-point, we'll all get out and flash our IDs. *Like hell we will!*'

But Pat McDowell shouted him down. 'Leave off, Jerry Hogan!' he yelled. 'You've done enough today.' Hogan spat into a corner and muttered under his breath, 'Well, we should dump him. We'd be better off dumping him now.'

'Dump him? Are you out of your tiny mind? So he can go running to the police?'

'Got any other suggestions?' Hogan sneered, out of the rattling darkness. Stan, all ears in his corner of the truck, knew what Jerry was playing at and it wasn't very clever. He'd shot his bolt with Michael and the Organization by trading Liam Boyle's life for Stan's, and even now he wanted to save him. But it must look like weakness to them, treachery even. That was why he'd hardened up towards him again. 'Well, have you?' he repeated.

'Only this,' Pat replied, running a finger along the snout of his pistol. 'It was all right for Liam Boyle. Or had you forgotten?'

Stan heard and a dullness crept through him; he was beyond surprises now. So they were going to shoot him anyway, if the rest of their great plan misfired. Killing the Brit was inevitable.

At last they were in the Republic. A code was tapped out through the cabin wall and Hogan crossed over to Peter who was still huddled at the tarpaulin, with his gun. That was sweet, Peter boy. Dint think it would be quite so easy,' he was fishing for his cigarettes as he talked. OK, let me take over. It'll be another hour before we stop. Get some kip if you want.' He pulled some sacks out from under Stan and pushed them at the McDowells. He can do without these, you have 'em.'

The twins looked at each other, then at Stan. Jerry Hogan was losing his grip, they'd seen right through his tough-guy act. What was he playing at?

'Changing your tune, aren't you?' Pat said. 'First you say let him go, now you're – '

'Belt up!' Hogan chopped him off in mid-sentence, stood up and looked through the slit in the tarpaulin. There's something following us. Tell Beatty.'

Peter tapped out a message on the cabin wall and they

heard the lorry rev wildly, then change gear. Suddenly the engine noise had become much louder. They were rocked violently from side to side as the driver got up speed. Everyone except Hogan sat down.

'Peter.'

The boy joined him at the slit. 'There's two of them, two cars. They must have picked us up at the border. Oh God.'

He crossed the floor and rapped with the handle of his gun on the cabin wall. 'Laffetty . . . can you hear me? *Laffetty!* Put your foot down, for God's sake. There's at least two vehicles, and there'll be somebody up front, along the road. For *Christ's sake!*'

He staggered back over the churning floor. Drums were rolling about from side to side, leaking petrol. He stared out. The darkness was slashed with white light. Over the rumble of the lorry there was a higher engine noise; they could hear the crunch of gears, brakes squealing on wet bends, then unmistakable, out of the darkness, gunfire.

They were all at the tarpaulin now. Stan, crouched down among a jumble of legs, peered too. He counted headlights before he ducked down into the sacking. Jerry was firing with both hands and the night rang with shots. The gunfire in the cabin smelt homely, like Bonfire Night.

The truck was going faster and faster now. Suddenly it started to jerk and lurch about violently, as if they were trying to cross a field of gigantic boulders. Then, quite abruptly, as the engine noise spluttered and began to die, Stan felt it turn over on its side and heard glass and metal showering into the road.

He screamed. Three figures, like black paper cut-outs in a line, passed through the gleaming slit into the open air. He could hear Hogan yelling, and a ripple of gun shot. Seconds later the cars behind stopped and there were men's voices, and dogs.

Then he smelled wet fields. Quite suddenly the dark seemed to have swallowed everything and the guns and voices were absorbed into the calm night over which a pale, round-faced moon presided peacefully.

But he couldn't free himself from the truck. His trouser-leg felt as if it was hooked on to something and he wrenched it all ways to get free. The slit was still visible, softly lit by the moon, but now it was horizontal and his clothing was wet. The lorry had been full of petrol cans. He tore madly at the invisible hook in the floor and realized as he struggled that the engine was still on, groaning and sparking like a sick mangled creature.

At last he tore himself free and leapt out of the truck, running crazily into the welcoming blackness. Seconds later there was an almighty explosion and the night was lit up as the old truck blazed cheerfully. But Stan was rolling over and over in a muddy lane, jerking like a crazy marionette as fire spread along his trouser-leg, towards his face.

When he opened his eyes he thought he must have died. He was swaying about gently and there was a very bright blue sky overhead. Two men, in robes of coarse brown cloth, roped at the waist, were bending over him anxiously. They wore black crucifixes round their necks.

He was being pushed along a bumpy track in something with high wooden sides that smelt strongly of geraniums. As they went inside out of the sun a cold museum smell met him. Somewhere quite near a choir was singing church music and a solitary muffled bell tolled high over his head.

Then pain. At first he thought his legs had been amputated, there seemed to be no sensation below his waist, but when he tried to move his whole body throbbed wildly, crying out to be left alone. He'd been badly scalded with boiling milk once, at Mrs Kelly's. This was that pain again but doubled and redoubled till he could hardly bear it. He moaned and tossed about; he must get away from the pain.

'Come on, lad, try to keep still,' a gentle voice said in his ear. 'We'll have you in bed in a minute. You'll be more comfortable in here surely.'

He was lifted out of the wheelbarrow and lowered carefully on to a high, hard mattress. Sheets were pulled up over him, cold and fresh-smelling, and they arranged them across a crude wooden-cage thing over his legs.

Chapter Nineteen

'OK, Stan, are you going to try and eat something for us today? You're a big lad, and you're still growing. You need more than milk, you know.'

Very slowly he opened his eyes and looked in the direction of the voice. At first there was a flood of brightness, light so intense it caused pain, bright gold turning peach, darkening to pinky-red. Then heads, blotched and blurred, that turned to faces as his vision grew steadier. Two men, in brown monks' robes, one an old tanned face, weathered down to crumpled leather, the other youngish, big-eared and comical, with bright eyes like chips of blue-stone.

'How d'you know my name?'

'Oh, you've been with us quite a while now,' the older man said. 'There's not much we don't know about you, Stan Mellor. Every day we get letters, and people come on the telephone. It's quite a fan club you've got.'

The voice was quiet and very kind but underneath the coarse sheets Stan shivered. Would Julius get him even here, in this peaceful place? Through half-closed eyes he could see the pointed face pressed against the high-barred grille in the wall, could hear the rat-like scrabbling.

'*Julius!*' He was half screaming.

'There's nobody here but us, Stan,' the old man said, putting his gnarled brown hand on the bedcover.

'Brother Aloysius here, and I'm Brother Benedict. You are quite safe here. Rest now.'

'Could you eat some broth?' The younger monk was looking down at him hopefully. 'Some broth and a bit of bread, perhaps? You need nourishment surely.'

'I'll have a go.'

Aloysius went off silently and closed the door on them.

'What happened to the others?' Stan said.

Brother Benedict screwed his eyes up and frowned slightly.

'What others, Stan – why don't we start at the beginning? You've had quite a time of it, haven't you, one way and another, since you left London? Why don't we –'

But Stan cut him short. He couldn't bear to go through it all, not yet, not even with this kind old man.

'I mean those boys in the lorry, that gang . . . when I got burned. You *know who I mean*!' He was half shouting, half weeping, and tossing his aching head from side to side, to rid his brain of the memory; the oily smell of the cab was in his nostrils and he could hear the sick juddering of the lorry over the stones, the final explosion. He was shaking violently.

'They put up a fight, but the police got them. Those that were left were taken into custody and charged.'

The monk made his knotted fingers into a web. He looked deep into it for a long time, not speaking. Then he looked at Stan.

The boy's mind was heavy, dull with sleep and the drugs a doctor had given him to kill the pain, but a flash of clear memory suddenly stabbed through him. He remembered the border.

'The *police*? But how could they? I thought we'd gone over the border? I thought when you'd crossed over like, you were safe?'

Brother Benedict sat silent again, then he said slowly, 'We're very near the border here, Stan, and in border

174

country there are certain arrangements made, just occasionally, now and again.'

'What do you mean, *arrangements*? Are you mixed up in the fighting too? Do monks work for the terrorists then? It doesn't sound very Christian to me,' and he turned his face away, towards the blank wall. All his life there'd been 'religious' people on his back and most of them had been a bit peculiar, miserable, like Auntie Marjorie, or hard and unyielding like the matron of one temporary care centre, and like old Vera Stott. Where did God come into it, and Jesus Christ? Christianity was supposed to be about love, and peace, not blowing people to bits. 'You in league with the IRA too then?' he said, through clenched teeth, but the tears were running down his cheeks. He kept thinking of Goblin Child, and the two shots, and the screaming. Liam Boyle had died because of him.

The deep silence of the place was marred only by Stan's broken voice. Gently the old monk leaned across the bed and brought the boy's head round to face him. 'Look at me, son,' he whispered. 'Don't doubt us. I understand a little of what you must feel, the shock of it all, the pain. Of course the fighting's nothing to do with us, except that we pray for those people, every day, like we pray for you.'

'But you said "arrangements",' Stan repeated, letting the old man dry his eyes for him with a big handkerchief, 'as if you knew what was going on. What did you mean?'

'Only that the police work together sometimes, in remote country places like this where people slip across the border. The Garda had been alerted about your gang. That's all I mean.'

'It wasn't "my gang",' Stan whispered. 'I got into it by accident, it was just a fluke. What happened to them anyhow? Where are they all?'

'Well, there was a very long chase. Two of them managed to get away, brothers I think they were. They stole a van and headed south. But they got lost, and it was on the border that the police got them. Ironic, wasn't it, how it all worked out finally? They didn't know they were in fact heading back into Ulster, in all the confusion.'

He stopped and looked at Stan, half-smiling to reassure him. But the boy was staring ahead stonily.

'*The ones that got away* – there were five of them, two in the front of the lorry and three in the back, where I was. And the lorry caught fire.'

'I know. We saw it when we found you. The two in the cabin died, and afterwards one of the others, in the shooting. He wouldn't give in, not even when it became hopeless and the others had slipped away. He stayed there. Hogan his name was. Poor soul.'

Just for a minute Stan felt glad. There was a large painted crucifix on the bare wall of the cell. The face and body of the Christ were greenish-white and blood was painted liberally on the hands and feet. Liam's goblin face swam across it suddenly and Stan could hear his little girl's voice, *Ah, don't, Jerry.*

'He killed somebody,' he said, 'a boy called Liam Boyle who was sticking up for me. I heard the shots. They were going to leave me in the house when it got blown up, but Liam cut through the ropes and Jerry saw him. So he turned on him. He didn't know what to do, I could see that, and he let me go with the others even though the man at their headquarters had told him not to. But then he shot that boy Liam. He was begging him not to do it, but he did. It was me they should've killed, all along.'

Now he'd started to talk Stan couldn't stop. He was living through the horror of it all over again. He put his face in his hands and sobbed loudly.

Brother Benedict put his arms round him and cuddled him as though he were only little. 'I know, Stan, I know. But it's all right now. Everything's going to be all right now.'

*

The door opened and jug-eared Aloysius came in with a tray. The two men sat either side of the bed and helped him eat the broth. It was very good, full of barley and onions with a strong herby taste. They soaked some of the bread in it too so he could suck it up more easily, he felt so weak.

'Mrs Kelly used to make this kind of bread,' Stan sniffed, 'she was Irish as well.'

The two men exchanged glances. 'Yes. We've spoken to her brother today,' Aloysius said. 'He's called Joe Monagan, isn't he? They've got a farm outside Balycleuth. Your brother's there. It's Sid, isn't it?'

Stan was tired again after the eating and his mind felt dull, groping helplessly with shreds of fact as they danced about, always out of reach.

'It's Mr Kelly on the farm, Mrs Kelly's brother.'

'No, Stan, she *married* a Kelly. Her maiden name was Monagan, Eileen Monagan. We went to the same school,' Benedict added. 'You can't believe that I suppose, but it's true. She was a grand girl, Eileen was.'

Of course, *Monagan* not *Kelly*.

'I'm stupid,' Stan said aloud. 'I got on the wrong boat.'

Aloysius went off with the tray and Benedict smoothed Stan's sheets down carefully. 'I should try to go to sleep now, Stan. Sleep as long as you can, it's the best cure. When you feel like talking tell Aloysius. We've asked him to look after you. The doctor'll be in and out, of course, and there'll be a couple of other people coming along to see you, in a few days. Not till you feel more yourself though.'

'Policemen?'

'I believe so. They have to come, Stan. They need to get a few facts from you.'

'Will they take me back to England?'

'I don't know. But they've been in touch with your brother at Balycleuth. It sounds hopeful to me. I can't tell you any more than that. Don't worry about it just now.'

Stan didn't ask any more, but he felt suspicious. He saw the whole of his journey with all its pains and terrors, its nightmares, its touches of sweetness, all shrunk down to a few cold sentences on an official sheet, and a return ticket slapped down on top of it. They always got runaway boys in the end, and brought them back. They'd get him. He felt cold, hard inside. It was as if nothing good was ever going to happen again.

There was a bleakness over everything now, a terrible empty feeling. When he'd started off, in London, he'd been in control of events, at the centre. It hadn't exactly been plain sailing but at least he'd ordered his own movements. No one had pushed him around since he'd first hit the road. Now it was all different and he felt himself and his concerns somehow eclipsed, almost petty. Liam Boyle, who had tried to save him, had been killed in cold blood and three more of them afterwards, in the shoot-out. They'd not died for fun but for the 'free Ireland' Liam had told him about and because of those long, agonized centuries of bloody history. When he thought about it Stan felt shrunken and small and his own journey to Ireland, such a vast undertaking to him, seemed an irrelevance.

'You're keen on football, aren't you, Stan?'

'How d'you know that?'

'As I said, there's a lot we know, now,' the old monk said, getting slowly to his feet. 'Some of us follow the football here, though rugby's the great Irish game. I'd like to know who you think's got the best chance in the First Division.'

Stan wasn't listening. Football and rugby had no place in this harsh world he inhabited now. The bloody crucifix danced in front of him as faintness made his vision weak and blurry. 'Brother Benedict,' he called out. The old man, half-way through the door, turned back.

'Yes, Stan?'

'Would it be all right if you took that cross down. I can't stand it.'

When he eventually dozed off he was out for ten hours. He felt fresher, more alert when he came round again. Sunshine was pouring in through the high cell window and Brother Aloysius was standing on a stool opposite the bed, tacking up a coloured poster. The blood-stained crucifix had gone and in its place was a small gilt-framed picture of the Virgin and Child.

The monk stepped down from the stool and admired the poster.

'He's grand, that one. Do you not agree, Stan?'

Stan inspected Ian Rush in profile, the big handsome nose, the dark moustache.

'I don't know, really,' he said doubtfully. 'I think he's going off, sometimes. Where did you get it from?'

'From the sports shop in town. I went specially. Oh, and there are these letters for you, and a newspaper.'

He put everything on the bed. Stan didn't want to see the paper, in his dreams and in his nightmares he was still a boy on the run, but he picked the two envelopes up. They were both from London; he studied the dates.

'They came some time ago, but you weren't well enough. Now the Abbot thought perhaps . . .'

'How long have I been here then?'

'Nearly two weeks. You started off in our little infirmary. You don't remember, do you?'

Stan shook his head. 'Why didn't they put me in a hospital?' he asked.

Aloysius grinned. 'We are miles from a hospital here. You could have been admitted, of course, because of your legs, but the Abbot persuaded the police, and the doctor. We wanted you to stay here with us, we believed that would be better for you.'

'Why?' said Stan, but something had already told him the answer. Hospitals meant officials and official questions. If he'd been carted off to a hospital it'd have meant going backwards, things closing in on him again, an end to his great expedition to freedom, to Sid and the little Irish farm. He sensed that these monkish men knew more about him and his longings than he'd actually told them, and what they didn't know they seemed to understand in their hearts. They were simple people and they were good. He wished Auntie Marjorie could meet them, and Vera Stott. What they believed seemed to fill them with a sort of quiet joy.

He said, 'What about the burns though? How bad are they?' He'd not yet seen himself without any clothes on, he only knew about the pain.

Aloysius shrugged. 'Your legs look pretty nasty when I change the dressings, but they're not nearly as bad as they look, according to the doctor. You're young, and you've got grand healing flesh. The scars will fade. Those boots you had saved your feet, marvellous they are. I've never seen such boots.'

He turned round and pointed at a low wooden chest where Stan's clothes were in a neat pile with the boots on top, carefully shined up by somebody.

'They belonged to an old man called Jack. His widow gave them to me in Warrington. She was great, she was. I'd like to see her again. She must think I cheated her, and I didn't. I had to take money off her, but I want to give it back. Do you think – '

'You can put it right, Stan, when you're up and on your feet again. But I should think you're after getting down to Balycleuth first, aren't you?'

'Sid knows then?'

'We told you, yes. The police have been in touch with the Monagans. He's been waiting for you, for two weeks.'

'Do they want me there though?' Stan whispered.

'I'll leave you to read your letters,' the monk replied, tiptoeing away.

They were from Miss Dobbs and Auntie Marjorie. Miss Dobbs's was a funny one, all about school. She said she missed him in her lessons and that the school soccer team was falling apart without him. She was getting married at Easter and they were touring Ireland on their honeymoon. 'Could we come and see you?' she scribbled at the end. There was nothing about his journey, or about Victor, or about Belfast, nothing to suggest he wasn't staying where he was, now he'd made it. She ended the letter 'Dear Stan, we're all so glad you're all right. I always knew you'd do something remarkable!' and in the envelope was a big Snoopy get-well card that everyone in the class had signed.

Auntie Marjorie's letter was much more business-like but she didn't mention his journey either. She just said she was very glad he was OK and that she'd like to come and see him when she'd sorted her move out. She didn't mention Victor either, only that she was moving up North to live near her sister, and that Kingsley and Elspeth were coming as well. So they'd be living in the country too. She enclosed a five-pound note.

Stan lay in bed turning the money over in his fingers. His eyes filled with tears.

'Are you all right, Stan?' Aloysius had come back, with some milk in a beaker.

He nodded and rubbed at his face. 'Auntie Marjorie sent me this. I wish she hadn't. She never has any money to spare.'

'Why don't you write to her?'

'I will. I'll write to her first. I suppose they could put her up at the farm, couldn't they, if she came to see me?'

The police visited him two days later though they weren't in uniform. They both wore discreet ties, dark suits and had very glossy shoes. 'Special Branch' Aloysius explained afterwards. Chairs were put by the bed for them, and tea and sandwiches were brought on a tray.

'We're not going to ask you a lot of questions, Stan,' the older man, Derek Oliver, said at once. 'We've pieced together your story, and the Abbot gave us this. It was quite helpful.'

Stan looked. In his outstretched hand, rolled up small and grubby in a rubber band, was his red Woolies' notebook.

'This tells us quite a bit, Stan. You wrote all your movements down, the dates and everything. Why, I wonder?'

He wasn't exactly smiling but his face was calm. Instinctively, Stan trusted it.

'Why do you want to know?'

'I think it's unusual. I know how the idea started, it was at school, wasn't it?'

'Did Miss Dobbs tell you?'

'She did. She also told us you were one of her best pupils.'

Miss Dobbs. Stan had almost forgotten her, until he'd read her letter. So Miss Dobbs knew everything. What must she think of him now?

'It didn't work out as I'd planned,' he said. 'I'd saved up. If someone on the motorway hadn't stolen my money it'd have been all right. I didn't want to steal from anyone. But what else could I do?'

The detective inspector's assistant was busy scribbling down everything Stan said.

'Why's he doing that?' he said suspiciously. 'Do I have to go to court?'

'*Stan.* Nobody's going to charge you with anything. These notes are just for the record. Relax . . . you were telling us about your notebook.'

'It all went wrong. I had to go into a shop and steal some food and then, in Warrington this old lady was nice to me, really kind, and her sister said prayers. And then . . . and then . . .'

But the tears were coming again, worse than before. Stan thought he would go mad. He was turning into a soft kid that turned the tap on at the least thing. But inside him it was like a great sea, rising, turning over and crashing down, threatening to swamp him. The sisters had liked him, trusted him, and he couldn't bear to think of them going into the front room, finding the window open and the money pinched from the copper kettle.

'I cheated them, I admit, but I had to get on the boat. I had to. So I just cleared off. If only Julius – '

'Julius Lodge?' Derek Oliver's voice hardened slightly. Stan nodded then said, 'Did they get him?'

'Yes. He was arrested when he got off the ferry, with someone else, a young man they thought might be you. The boy was released after questioning, of course, but they couldn't take any chances.'

'Where's Julius now?' The uncertainty made Stan feel sick. As long as Julius Lodge was free he could not rest.

'In London, Stan. He's awaiting trial, like his friend Victor. They'll be inside for a good long stretch, this time.'

The assistant was looking back through his notebook. He said, 'Lodge told us you threw his package into the sea. Is that right?'

Stan nodded.

'Why did you do that, Stan? You know what it was I suppose?'

'Drugs, wasn't it? It must've been.'

'Heroin. It was part of a record haul. The whole lot was worth over two million.'

'Did Lodge go for you after you threw it over the side?' Derek Oliver leaned forward keenly.

'No – no,' Stan said firmly. The episode was painted on his memory. 'When he saw it go he started to cry.'

There was silence in the white sunlit cell.

'Why did you throw it away, Stan?'

'I dunno. I suppose I panicked. I suppose I thought if I got rid of it he might leave off me.'

But it wasn't that. If it hadn't been for the drugs Julius would never have gone after him in the first place, and without Julius things wouldn't have gone wrong. He wouldn't be lying here with the skin off his legs, being questioned as if he were a sort of criminal. At the beginning he'd been his own man, and sure of himself. Julius Lodge had dirtied him. He'd turned him into a cheat and a thief.

The two men got up to leave. 'Have you got anything to ask us, Stan?' Derek Oliver was standing over him, offering his hand. 'Anything we can help with?'

Stan had turned his face away from them. They'd been kind enough, in their remote, official way, but he felt strangely bitter. 'I don't suppose you'd have bothered with me if it hadn't been for Julius and Victor, would you? That's why you came, isn't it?' he asked them. He wanted to say, Nobody's interested in me for myself, it's only because I got mixed up with the great Julius Lodge.

They were embarrassed. Derek Oliver said, 'We were sent here by headquarters, Stan. We're just doing our job, that's all. And we wish you all the best from now on.' They both shook his hand as it lay limp on the bed-cover, and turned to go.

'Will I be sent back?' Stan asked as they went through the door.

'We just can't say. That's for other people to decide, I'm afraid. Good luck, though.'

'Thanks.'

But when they had gone and the door was shut, Stan buried his face in the pillow and wept as if his heart would break.

Chapter Twenty

Brother Benedict took him down to Balycleuth in the Abbot's car. It was an old Morris Minor Estate, the kind with a polished wooden frame. Stan had helped them to clean it, before setting off. They were pleased when he explained that it was a 'classic' car, the sort people were starting to collect. 'We've had it for years,' Aloysius told him. 'It still goes well, so we keep it. But people always have to buy new things, don't they? I think it's sad, when the old things have served them faithfully.' Stan liked that. He was going to miss this quiet place and its simple, quiet men.

The old monk drove very cautiously but even so he felt every rut and bump. His legs still had dressings on but he'd practised walking about in the monastery garden and he could manage quite well now, in spite of the long days in bed. They'd lent him a stick, though, to steady himself.

The journey down into County Cork took most of the day, along wild empty roads. Much of the time Benedict drove straight down the middle. They saw cars and lorries in towns but the countryside was full of animals, wandering about all over the place. He stopped several times to coax chickens and sheep out of the way, sitting there quite patiently with the sun on his crumpled brown face. People on bicycles waved at them as they pedalled by. On and off Benedict hummed quietly to himself, bits of hymns and old jigs in Irish. Stan dozed between the bumps, he still felt more in a dreamworld than in the middle of 'real life' and he fell asleep rather easily these days. Aloysius had told him he was getting to be a real old man.

It was past four o'clock when they began to creep up a steep hill and he got his first sight of the sea. To their right was a low stony hillock with sheep in the foreground, and at the end of a long windy track he could see a clutter of untidy whitewashed buildings. Benedict pipped his horn twice and a tractor in a higher field stopped its engine. Somebody waved to them and a blue speck got out and began to move rapidly downhill, towards the farm. They turned into the open gateway and steered carefully down the muddy lane.

Stan got out of the car and hobbled up to the door on his stick. This was the moment he'd imagined for so long, but nothing was as he'd planned. He was weak and tottery, now he was on his feet again, and he'd lost a lot of weight. His hair looked funny too, all sticking out with the curls only half grown back after Mary's efforts with the scissors. Aloysius had found him some old shorts to wear, so that nothing would irritate the bandages; he looked ridiculous.

He moved painfully up the path to the farmhouse door and went in. Three people materialized out of corners and came up to meet him, then everyone froze in embarrassment, not knowing what to say.

Old Joe Monagan's weather-beaten face was just like Mrs Kelly's. There was no mistaking the likeness and, for a moment, Stan felt pain, it brought her so close. Then he was glad. The farmer shuffled forward awkwardly, uncomfortable in a shirt and tie, pulling at his collar. He took Brother Benedict's hand briefly – they knew each other too, from the old days – then he hugged Stan. It was as if he'd come home like a long-lost son. Mrs Monagan hugged him too, standing on her toes; she was little and dumpy with wisps of grey hair escaping from a bun. She seemed very flustered by the sudden silence in the farm kitchen and soon went back to her cooker where two large kettles were boiling.

'It's all ready,' she said, 'so just sit down, everybody. Joe, get a chair for Benedict, will you.'

The long table was laid for tea with what looked like the very best china and three different kinds of cake. Stan sat down on an old settle by the fireplace and the girl who'd got up to greet him came and sat there too. 'Hallo, Stan, I'm Maraid, Sid's girlfriend. We've been getting ready for you all day. So how are you keeping now?'

'Oh, all right, thanks,' he said shyly. She was pretty, very dark with thick brown hair, about eighteen perhaps. Sid liked good-lookers.

He came in suddenly, with a great rush, knocking over a bucket. He'd got eyes for nobody but his kid brother. Stan lifted his face nervously, afraid that it would all be different, afraid he'd just be an embarrassment, *afraid*. Then they looked at one another for a very long time. Sid was even taller now, and handsomer, his hair a great tangle of curls under the old bob-cap he wore for driving the tractor.

He stared down without smiling at the thin pale boy on the old settle, taking in the crazy hair-do, the white face, the bandages. Then he just said '*Stan*,' bent down and wrapped his arms round him.

At the table nobody talked much to him, and nobody referred to Julius or the gang, or anything else that had happened. It was as if he'd merely dropped in for a cup of tea, while he was passing the door. Benedict chatted to Joe and his wife about childhood days in Balycleuth and Sid told Stan all about farming. He'd not given it up yet then!

Maraid kept offering him plates but Stan couldn't eat

much, he felt too nervous, too unsure of himself and where he was going to fit in. She was nice, Maraid, she kept teasing Sid about his appetite and about being so untidy. 'Mrs Monagan's giving you his room, Stan,' she told him. 'You can see the sea from it. He's moving into the one at the back. It's smaller – not so much to fill with rubbish.' And she poked him. 'I'm trying to reform him before we get married.'

Ah yes, thought Stan, Sid had always gone for the girls. Maraid would make a fabulous wife too.

'Your Sid tells me you've got all the brains,' she went on. 'Will you be going to the Academy, in Balycleuth?'

Stan hesitated and looked at the floor. 'I don't know,' he muttered. 'I mean I don't really know what's happening, if I'm staying or not.'

'Of course you're staying, don't be so *thick*. I tidied up my bedroom specially,' and Sid pushed at him, across the tea table. Benedict and Joe exchanged swift glances and went on talking about the new Irish full-back who'd been in all the papers. But Mrs Monagan put a hand on his shoulder. 'I'll take you upstairs in a minute, Stan,' she whispered. 'I expect you're a bit tired. Just let me top up the teapot.'

She led the way up some stone stairs and down a long dark passage. It was cooler away from the kitchen and he could smell lavender furniture polish. Everything was very clean and all the bedroom doors were open to the sunlight.

'This room's on the small side but I hope it'll do. Maraid's a good girl, she helped clear it out for you. Your Sid's after having the little back room now, it was his own idea. He thought you'd like this one better. He's grand, your Sid is,' she said approvingly, as she stood in the doorway, clasping and unclasping her hands.

The bedroom wasn't much bigger than his cell at the monastery and these walls were white too. But there was a bright red rug by the bed, and red cotton curtains.

Through the open window, beyond a green hump, Stan saw the sea.

He sat down on the bed, suddenly weary. 'It's great, Mrs Monagan, it's really great. But am I actually staying? I mean, do *you* know anything? The police came to see me, at the monastery, but they didn't say what was happening. They said they didn't *know*.'

The dumpy little woman looked at him rather nervously. 'Joe'll tell you what's been said, Stan, when we get downstairs. I'm sure nothing's been decided yet, nothing definite anyway, surely.' She seemed a bit more relaxed away from the tea table, now they were on their own. 'I'm sure nothing will be sorted out for a week or so yet,' she added, 'not till your Auntie Marjorie comes over and that. But, for now, well of *course* you're staying, it's a little holiday for you,' and she patted his knee reassuringly.

'A little holiday', with his tangled dreams full of bombs and blood, his nightmare about Julius Lodge splitting his head open with an iron bar, Liam Boyle in pieces on a filthy floor. *Ah, don't, Jerry*, that pathetic little voice. Would it ever stop haunting him, the terrible sound of it?

He said, 'I'm just wondering if you want me here, you being so busy and everything. It's all . . . so mixed up, now. It all went wrong, after I left London, the gang and everything, you know . . . my legs . . .' and he stopped. Words were too hard for him still and the tears were building up in his throat. But he mustn't cry here, not now, not any more; he prayed for calmness to the God of Auntie Marjorie, and Vera, and the monks.

'*Stan.*' Mrs Monagan's voice sounded much firmer, almost severe. 'Of course we want you here, now don't you say such things. Joe never forgot you and your brother, after Eileen passed away. Sid came over here, just like he always said he would, and he's doing quite well

189

at the farming. There was always a place for you too, when the time came.'

'And now I've come,' he said numbly.

'Yes, dear. And now you've come.'

'Well I hope they don't send me back to London, Mrs Monagan. I don't think I could stand London again. I'd like to stay here, for a bit, anyhow.'

'I believe that they'll *let* you stay, dear, once they've seen the place, and talked to me and Mr Monagan. I will pray to God they'll not send you back,' she added simply, flicking a corner of her apron at some non-existent dust. 'Now I'm going back to see how they're getting on with their tea. Come down when you're ready. Do you eat as much as Sid? You look as if you need building up a bit, to me. The bathroom's at the end of the passage.'

'I'll go and stand outside for a minute, if you don't mind,' Stan said. 'I feel a bit queer.'

'Just as you like, dear. I'll go down.'

At the bottom of the stone stairs he found a cool flagged corridor that ran from front to back of the house. He went along it, creeping slowly past the kitchen door, trying not to knock against anything with his stick, and let himself out into the yard.

It was better in the fresh air with a gust blowing in from the sea, salty and fresh. Stan took great gulps of it and his head stopped spinning.

He considered everything. First, he'd been made really welcome. Sid, Maraid, the Monagans, everyone had welcomed him, there was no doubt about that. And they must all feel for him, because of what had happened; he knew that because nobody had talked about it. They'd been watching each other though, and him, but not in a disapproving way.

They'd said they wanted him to stay too, so that was all right, though what would happen when Auntie

Marjorie came over he just wasn't sure. There must be all sorts of 'rules' about people like him, his whole life had been 'rules'. He wouldn't expect too much, too soon. There was no point.

Whatever they decided he was on his own now and he was going to have to make his own way. In the end he'd been dead lucky, everyone round him being kind, treating him like a piece of bone china after the dance he'd led them. But they all had their own lives to lead and he must carve out his own patch; nobody would do it for him.

Sid and Maraid were obviously going to get married. That meant a move to their own place, and children. If it all worked out as he hoped, and they didn't send him back to London, perhaps he could stay here with the Monagans. Not for ever though, they were getting old.

He hoped Auntie Marjorie would bring Elspeth with her, she'd love this farm. He could just see her perched up on the tractor with Sid, fussing over all the cats, feeding the hens with Mrs Monagan. He tried not to think of the Elspeth he'd left behind, frightened and dirty, waking up in her little cubby-hole to find big Stan had deserted her and run away to Ireland. He wanted to make up for everything because she was his flesh and blood. Someone of his own, like Sid.

The yard was paved with white concrete slabs. It had been a cloudless sunny day and the heat still rose up from it, beating him in the face. He stared down at his feet. In the crumbs of soil between the squares something had taken root. A clump of nameless weeds, yellow-green and shrivelled, stood up strongly against the wind like the crest on a Roman helmet.

It was October already and they would die off soon. Soon, all that was left of them would be rubbed away to a brownish powder. But in early spring they would come again, a line of green, then a few shoots, and at last another tiny thicket that would bud and flower and scatter its seeds.

They had survived, pushing up strongly through the concrete slabs, into the light and the rain. Nobody had helped them and yet, surely, they would go on. Stan looked at the small shoots. He also would endure, like them.